Broken Limits
The Limit: Book Three

CASTLE VIEW PRESS

Copyright © 2022 by Marissa Farrar and S R Jones.

All rights reserved.

No portion of this book may be reproduced in any form without written permission from the publisher or author, except as permitted by copyright law.

Edited by Lori Whitwam

Proofread by Jessica Fraser

Published by Castle View Press

If you'd like a super smutty retelling of one of the scenes from the guy's POVs, then grab it here and sign up to Marissa and Skye's newsletters at the same time!
https://BookHip.com/DAGCKZV

Chapter One
Honor

THE SCENT OF SALT CUTS through the air and, beneath me, the small white boat rises and falls with the ocean swell. The island is at my back, but though I could probably swim the distance between its shores and the boat, it might as well be another world away.

"Oh, you're not going back to the resort."

The male voice that has chased me through my nightmares for months is swiftly joined by a body as my stepfather—Detective Don Bowen—climbs out of the cabin.

"No!" I gasp.

I'm shaking hard, though that could be from either fear or the chill that's setting in. My clothes are damp from a combination of sweat and the misting rain. My boots and the lower part of my legs are soaking from wading through the shallows.

It's almost dark now, but I can clearly make out my stepfather's face by the lights of the boat.

I guess it's because of the time I spent with Wilder and Rafferty—both of whom are well into their thirties—that my stepfather suddenly doesn't seem so old to me anymore. The gulf of the years between us melts away, and, suddenly, I understand what my mother saw in him. His eyes are neither brown nor green, but a combination of both—brown at the center with emerald flecks at the edges. His hair is almost black, oiled like a raven's wing, with just a few sprays of white at the temples. His full lips are curled in a snarl. The lines around the corners of his eyes add to his maturity—a man aging like fine wine.

Had she been so blinded by his looks that she'd missed what a creepy son of a bitch he is? I imagine how his colleagues must treat him down at the station—hero worshiping him, the men wanting to be him, the women wanting to fuck him. It suddenly occurs to me that it's highly unlikely he was even faithful to my mother during their relationship. I'm not just thinking that because of how he looks. Men like him take what they want without caring how it might hurt someone else. There's a word for it—narcissistic.

I take a step back, only to collide with the solid body of Edwardo, the man I'd thought worked for the resort, but I'm now assuming works for someone else entirely. He might not understand what's happening here or who he's working with, though, so there's a possibility he could be an ally.

I spin around to face him. "Please," I beg. "Take me back to shore."

Edwardo shakes his head. "No can do, miss."

"He's going to kidnap me. He might even kill me. Please, I need your help."

Don's voice sounds from over my shoulder. "Edwardo has been informed of your part in all this. You won't be getting away this time."

I turn back to him. "What are you talking about?"

"You'll face the charges brought against you. No more running."

My jaw drops. "Charges? What charges?"

"Don't play the innocent with me. You're wasting your breath. You've been charged with multiple counts of possession of cocaine with intent to supply. Skipping your court hearing and going on the run wasn't a sensible thing to do. You should have known we'd track you down in the end."

It occurs to me that Edwardo might also be a cop, and that he's been lied to about what they're doing here.

"I'm not a drug pusher. I've never even tried drugs!"

I might have had a couple of tokes on a joint at a party, but it doesn't feel as though that counts right now.

I go back to begging for help from Edwardo. "Don is my stepfather. That's why he's here. He's the one who should be arrested! He killed my mother."

Don tuts and shakes his head. "See what those drugs have done to her? They've messed with her head. She has no idea what she's saying."

Tears fill my eyes. "I'm not on drugs. I know exactly what I'm saying."

Don reaches behind him and produces a set of handcuffs. If he gets those things on me, it's game over.

Desperately, I look back to shore. Though the boat hasn't moved in the short time that I've been on it, land suddenly feels a frighteningly long way away. It's almost dark, too. I pray that I'm going to spot Wilder or Rafferty, or Asher, or hell, even Brody, somewhere on the beach or through the trees above, but the place remains empty.

They'll have noticed I'm missing by now and will be searching for me. I'm sure of it. Maybe they'll see or hear the boat and realize what's happened and will come after me. Thank God they at least know about Don. I'd be completely screwed if they hadn't found out about him. At least now, there's the chance of them finding me again.

If that's what they want.

My stomach knots at the possibility they might be glad to see the back of me. I've caused so much trouble for them since I've been here—they might decide they'd rather I was gone.

Don lifts the handcuffs, as though to tease me with them and gives them a shake. "You gonna make this easy or hard?"

I refuse to make things easy for him. I'll swim back to shore if I have to. There is no way in hell I'm going to let my stepfather take me. I'm exhausted, starving, and dying of thirst but somewhere, deep inside of me, I find that final reserve of energy.

I lunge for the side of the boat, fully prepared to be submerged in the cool ocean and then swim like I've never swam before, but arms wrap around me, pinning me in place. I recognize the scent of him—musk mixed with an old-fashioned body spray like Lynx.

My stepfather is a big man, but he can move quickly when needed. His arms are bulked with muscle that can only have come from many hours spent in the gym, and his chest is solid at my back. I scream and thrash, but he hauls me off my feet, so I end up only kicking out at air.

"Calm down, bitch. Don't make me hurt you."

He's going to hurt me at some point—that much I'm sure of. He might not want to do it right in front of his colleague, but he will the moment we're alone.

Right now, he's still playing his 'cop' persona, but that won't last.

Something else occurs to me. Don is most likely armed.

My gut twists, and my prayer for the guys to appear on the beach goes up in smoke. What if they try to save me and Don shoots them? The thought delivers ice straight through my veins. If any of them get hurt because I've brought Don to their door, I'll never forgive myself.

I don't quit struggling, though, even as he wrenches my arms behind my back. I scream and manage to kick behind me, my booted foot making contact with his shin.

"Fuck! Bitch!" he snarls.

He yanks my arms hard, and pain shoots through my shoulders. It won't matter how many times I manage to kick him; he's too strong for me to break free. That doesn't mean I don't take immense satisfaction in the kick that did meet its mark, however.

The cold metal catches around my wrists and snaps into place.

"There," he says, finally letting go of me. "Now you're not going anywhere. If you try to swim, you'll drown."

He's right. I will. But isn't that a better way of dying than letting Don do whatever he wants with me? I wonder how much he knows about the island and the resort it houses and the four men who own it.

"How did you find me?" I dare to ask.

He arches an eyebrow. "Does it matter?"

I grit my jaw and glare at him. "Yes, 'cause then I'll know to avoid doing the same thing next time."

That elicits a chuckle from deep in his chest. "Next time? There won't be a next time. This is the last you'll see of freedom, probably for the rest of your life."

I'm aware he's still in cop mode and won't say out loud what he really intends to do with me, so I say it for him. "Why? Because you're planning to rape and murder me, just like you did to my mother?"

"No, because you're going to be spending the rest of your life behind bars, you little junkie whore." He looks to his colleague. "Edwardo, let's get moving."

Edwardo nods and passes by us, ducking into the cabin to go to the wheelhouse at the bow. I hate that it means I'm now left alone with Don. A moment later, the engine roars to life and smoke filters across the water.

We're moving now, the boat bouncing across the waves. In the burgeoning darkness, the island grows smaller, and the cove I was picked up from vanishes altogether.

Tears fill my eyes, and I'm drowning in regret. If only I'd made some different choices. I should never have run from Brody. I'd let him do whatever he wanted to me a thousand times over rather than be stuck in the situation I am now. I should have just sucked his cock and spread my legs for him and let him take whatever hole he wanted. It wasn't as though I didn't care for Brody—I did, despite how he'd treated me recently. I understood that his actions stemmed from fear. And fucking Brody was always a fun experience. He knew exactly what to do with his hands, mouth, and cock. I should have just taken whatever punishment would have made him feel better and gone back to the others.

But then I shake my head at myself. No. I'd needed to stand up for myself. Brody had to understand that he couldn't take his fears out on me. He'd wanted me to leave—or at least that's what he'd convinced himself. That was why he'd done what he had. He'd been trying to make me quit.

It's with a bitter sweetness that I realize he got what he wanted. Is he happy now? Maybe it's bad of me, but I hope he isn't. I hope he's beating himself up with the understanding that we could have all had something truly unique and special, if only he'd gone with it.

"Where are you taking me?" I ask Don. "And don't say prison, because we both know that's bullshit. You're only saying that as a cover to ensure you've got one of your colleagues here to do your dirty work for you."

Don spits air from between his teeth. "What's the point in you knowing where we're going? Are you hoping to find a phone and call someone for help?"

I don't know any of the numbers for the island off by heart. They'd been programmed into my phone, which is still in my locker. I know my best friend's number, but there's no way I'd phone her and risk pulling her into this mess. I love Ruth too much to ever do that to her. Then there's the police, but it's not like I can call them. The reason for that is staring directly at me. These people protect their own, and I know they'll take Don's side if I report him. I tried to do it once before, right after my mother died, and I was accused of being hysterical.

"No, but aren't I allowed to be curious about what my future holds for me?"

He falls silent, and then his eyes narrow. "Something seems different about you, but I can't quite put my finger on it."

I remain silent and sullen. If my arms weren't cuffed behind my back, I'd have folded them across my chest. I *am* different. I'm not that naïve girl anymore. I wonder what Don would make of Rafferty, Wilder, Asher, and Brody, if he were to come face to face with them. How could he not be intimidated by four such men? But then I remember he's most likely armed and force the thought out of my head in case I somehow manifest the scenario.

"What were you doing on that island, anyway?" he asks.

"Working," I mutter.

"What kind of work?"

"Cleaning rooms."

He raises an eyebrow. "You were a maid?" His gaze flicks up and down my body. "Seems like a waste, though I imagine you look good in the outfit."

I scowl. "Fuck you."

He seems to think of something and frowns. "What about the current getup, then?" He gestures to the Lara Croft outfit. "Not exactly something you'd clean in."

"It's practical."

I can't let Don know what kind of thing happens at the resort or on the island. If he even gets a clue that there's more going on than it just being an exclusive retreat for the very wealthy, he will do everything in his power to bring the business down. I imagine the ways he might do this—accusations of tax fraud, perhaps. Or will he hide drugs on the premises so he can bust them? I won't put anything past him. He's capable of manipulating every situation to suit what he wants.

A part of me—some crazy, wild, reckless part—wants to tell Don exactly what I've been up to. I want to see his face as I describe what I've been letting four men do to me over this past week. I want to tell him how they've used my body in ways that he could only ever dream of, and that I've loved it. I've loved having their cocks in my ass and mouth and pussy, sometimes all at the same time. I've loved being covered in their cum and still wanting more. I've loved having their tongues and fingers inside me. What I won't tell him is how much I've grown to care for them all—even Brody—as well. I won't tell him how the bond we've created has somehow become something more than physical.

My heart aches.

Will I ever see them again?

I'm sure they'll have come out searching for me when they realized I'm missing. How long will it take them to come to the understanding that I'm not on the island at all? What if they think I've run? If Brody tells them what happened between us, they might come to the conclusion that I couldn't handle it anymore and I finally tapped out.

But no, they understand how much I want—and need—that money. I would never leave without at least taking the two hundred grand that's owed to me. I'm pretty sure Rafferty will be certain of that. Then there's the practical side of things. How would I have even got off the island on my own? Once they check all their boats and discover none are missing, they're going to realize I wouldn't have tried to swim for it.

Unless they think I'd have done something stupid. No, they know I'm not suicidal. I would never have thrown myself off the side of a cliff into the ocean or anything like that.

But what if they decide it's an accident? That maybe I fell, and they're expecting my body to wash up onshore.

Tears fill my eyes once more, and I do my best to blink them away, not wanting Don to see any weakness about me. I want to have faith that this will somehow all work out, but my future looks as dark as the ocean beneath me.

Chapter Two
Rafferty

HONOR IS NO LONGER on the island.

We tracked her footsteps to the beach, where they vanished, and since none of our boats are missing, we can only conclude that someone has taken her.

That someone must be her stepfather.

Asher is standing in the middle of the room like stone, his fists clenched at his sides. His eyes aren't even focused on anything. He's lost inside his own head, probably picturing himself tearing the man who has taken Honor limb from limb. I know he's blaming himself for not disguising his search on Honor's real name properly, and so allowing her stepfather to find her, but it's not going to help her, or any of us, if he loses his shit.

He needs to focus that rage on something useful rather than turning it in on himself.

"Asher, get online," I tell him. "Do your thing. Find out everything you can about this man and where he might have taken Honor."

Brody speaks. "He'll have to dock the boat somewhere, most likely on the mainland. If we've caught the boat on camera as they leave, we'll get an idea what direction he's headed, at least."

I nod in agreement. "Good thinking."

I know we all just want to take off, to chase this asshole down and tear Honor out of his arms, but we'd be chasing our tails without doing the groundwork first.

Brody sits with his knuckles pressed to his lips. He's torturing himself, too.

I guess each of us is. It's just that some of us have more reason to than others.

"This wasn't your fault," I tell him. "You couldn't know she was going to get lost or that this stepfather of hers was going to track her down."

Brody's lips pinch tight. "I shouldn't have done it. I was jealous. What kind of fucking pussy gets jealous of a girl?" He shakes his head. "I scared her. I frightened her on purpose. I wanted to try to make her leave. This is my fault." He punches himself in the temple and knots his fingers in his hair. "Fuck. I'm a piece of shit. You should kick me off the island. It's what I deserve."

I stand in front of him and lean down to clasp his shoulder. "Brody, fucking stop it. If you want to make things right, then stop beating yourself up and do something practical to help find her."

He lifts his head to look at me, and I witness pain swirling in his eyes.

"Like what? She's gone. Just vanished into thin air."

"That's bullshit, and you know it. No one just vanishes. Whoever has taken her will have left a trail. The only way they could have gotten to the island is by boat, a seaplane, or a chopper. We'd have heard a seaplane or helicopter, so that only leaves a boat. They might have somehow hacked into our security system and killed the cameras on that coast, but that doesn't mean we won't have caught them on another camera."

Asher is sitting at the computer now, but he glances over his shoulder at us. "Rafferty is right."

Of course I am. "We know who this man is," I continue. "We know his name, his job. I bet we can even find out his home address and what kind of porn he likes to beat off to, if we put our minds to it."

Brody's tongue swipes across his lower lip. "Yeah, but will we find all that out before he does something to Honor?"

Wilder growls—actually growls like an animal. "If he lays a single fucking finger on her, I'll cut his balls off and shove them down his throat."

We're all left with that mental image, and none of us disagrees with him.

"While Asher is finding out what he can online," I say, "the rest of us need to get on the security footage from the last few hours and see what we can spot. Two cameras were out, but there are plenty of others we can check. Anything might be of help."

I can tell it's not what they want to be doing, but Brody and Wilder set themselves up to go back over the footage. I join them.

It's slow, monotonous work, and every minute that goes by puts more distance between Honor and us. We're not men who are good with sitting silently, when what we really want is to be moving and using our fists, but it's necessary.

Twenty minutes pass, and Wilder thumps his fist on the console.

"I've got something!"

The rest of us rise to stand behind him, allowing us to see his screen. It's the view from the most easterly point of the island. On the water, in the distance, is a small white blob. The boat.

I shake my head, pissed that none of us saw it earlier. If we had, we might have realized something was wrong. But it wasn't as though we didn't get boats passing the island. Sometimes, we even got dickheads taking it upon themselves to moor here, but we saw them off quickly enough.

"Can you blow that image up?" I ask. "There's a name on the side of the boat. If we can read it, it might be a lead."

Wilder turns to Asher. "This is your department, not mine."

The two men switch places.

"Give me two secs," Asher says.

He adjusts his glasses, then his fingers fly over the keyboard. The image fills the screen, then shifts and sharpens. We can see the text now but it's too distorted to read.

"Fuck." I drag my hand through my hair.

Asher shakes his head. "I'm not done yet."

He minimizes the window and pulls up another program, then imports the image into that. I don't know exactly what he's doing, but as Asher works, the name of the boat becomes legible.

"Got you," Asher says.

Secret Truth

I read it, and my heart thuds. The room seems to tilt.

"Does that mean anything to any of you?" I manage to say.

Brody frowns. "It's ringing a bell. Why do I know it?"

Wilder growls. "Isn't that something Pastor Wren used to say?"

I stare at it, ice running through my veins, chilling me, so the hairs on the back of my neck stand on end. It must be a coincidence. Nothing more than that. But I'm sick to my stomach, just as I always am when something reminds me of him and that time. I'm transported back to being a skinny kid, and the confusion and shame and guilt that comes with it.

I hate that man for doing what he did to us. And the four of us are most likely only a fraction of the boys he's abused over the years. We were so lucky to have found each other—or at least it wasn't luck but was down to Asher's computer-smarts. Wren is still out there, though, possibly still into adolescent boys. I hate that we haven't stopped him yet, but we're close now. Brody is right when he says Honor has been a distraction, and she continues to be a distraction, but we'll get there. I'm hoping that because of his age—he must be in his sixties by now—that his *urges* will have left him. But there are plenty of cases of men in their sixties fathering children, so it's not as though his age is guaranteed to put a stop to it.

"Aren't boats supposed to be named after women?" Brody says.

I narrow my eyes. "This one clearly isn't."

Asher sits back. "They're not always named after women. It's more that the boats themselves are supposed to be considered female. They can have names like *Sea Dancer*, or *Legacy*, or *Midlife Crisis*."

I arch my brow. "*Midlife Crisis*?"

Asher shrugs. "What I'm trying to say is that a boat can pretty much be called anything."

"You think it's just coincidence, then?"

He turns in his chair and holds my eye. "It has to be, doesn't it?"

Something else occurs to me. "What if we're making the wrong assumption? What if the reason the boat has that name is because it's Pastor Wren who's taken Honor, not her stepfather?"

He shakes his head. "Not possible."

"Isn't it? How can you be so sure?"

"Wren has no idea we've come together."

Brody speaks up. "What if he's found out? What if this is his way of keeping us quiet?"

I hold up both hands. "We've got no proof of that. The most likely answer is normally the right one. The name of the boat is just a coincidence, it has to be. We already know Honor's stepfather was looking for her, and that he'd taken time off work."

Asher spins back around to the computer screen. "The boat must be registered to someone. Let's find that out before we start making up scenarios in our heads. If we can find out who owns the boat, we might get a lead on where she's been taken."

I blow out a breath, glad we have Asher onboard.

He's right. We need to focus on the facts.

Chapter Three
Honor

AN HOUR OR SO HAS PASSED since I was taken.

Don has clearly gotten bored of me already, as he rises to his feet and calls out to Edwardo. "Shift switch, buddy. You can come and watch over our little junkie here."

I'm relieved he's had enough of me, at least for the minute. I don't know Edwardo in the slightest, but I reason that no one can be as bad as Don.

Perhaps unsurprisingly, I haven't been offered anything to eat or drink. The rain has stopped now, so I can't even put out my tongue to dampen it. I don't want to ask these men for anything, though. My stomach is hollow, and I'm still cold and damp. It would be very easy for me to fall into a well of self-pity right now, but I refuse to give up.

Don enters the wheelhouse, and a moment later, Edwardo steps back out. He keeps his head down, as though he doesn't want to meet my eyes. Does any part of him doubt Don's story?

He takes a seat on the bench a couple of feet away from me. "Do you have any water?" I ask. "I'm really thirsty."

He doesn't speak, but goes to a cooler, pops the lid, and delves inside. He pulls out a plastic bottle of water and carries it over to me.

"You're going to need to help me." I jangle my wrists and the cuffs. "I can't hold anything."

He sighs but cracks the lid and holds the bottle to my lips, tilting it up. Water passes over my dry tongue, and I gulp thirstily. Some escapes and dribbles down my chin, but it doesn't matter.

"Enough," he snaps and takes the bottle away.

I don't mind. I feel better already. The headache that had been threatening like an oncoming storm starts to retreat.

"Thank you," I say. I drop my voice a level. "What has he told you about me?"

"Just what I need to know."

I think of how, in hostage situations, you're supposed to make the kidnapper see you as a real person. This isn't exactly the same situation, but I hang on to the hope that I might be able to bring him onto my side.

"My name is Honor. I'm twenty-one years old. My best friend is called Ruth. I want to be a songwriter one day, maybe even a singer. I'm not sure. I loved my mom more than anything before she died. I don't do drugs, though I do love the occasional glass of cham—"

"Shut up."

I don't shut up. "Please. You must be able to see that this isn't normal. Would you normally do an arrest like this? I haven't been read my Miranda rights or anything."

His lips thin. "Don told me you're his stepdaughter and he doesn't want to do things by the book."

I beg him with my eyes. "And you think that's right?"

Edwardo shrugs. "You have a drug habit. I can understand him wanting to keep things to himself. You don't exactly make him look good, what with him being a cop."

"Do *you* think I have a drug habit? Do I really look like a junkie?"

To be fair, after running from Brody and hiking across the island in the rain, I'm not exactly looking my best. I'm not even completely sure what a drug addict looks like, apart from what I've been fed by television and the media. Images of track marks and bad teeth pop into my head.

"Not everyone who deals drugs looks like a meth-head," he replies.

I think, desperately. "Then check my record. You'll see there's no warrant out for my arrest."

Would it have been possible for Don to get a warrant for my arrest? I'm not exactly sure about the mechanisms for these things, but I believe he'd need to submit some sort of case to a judge, and they'd issue one. But what if he has a friend in the court? He might have a judge on his side or even one who's open to a bribe or two. I don't doubt that Don is capable..

Is it better that I end up behind bars than being dead? Without question, yes. At least in jail I still have a chance of proving my innocence. Something else occurs to me. Unless, of course, that's Don's plan to get rid of me. If he can bribe someone in court, no doubt that he'll have contacts with people inside as well. The police aren't well-liked people in jail, but there will always be snitches and those either willing to take a bribe or who are even susceptible to being threatened. Perhaps they have loved ones on the outside whose lives are being threatened if they don't do as they're told. It would be a good way for Don to get rid of me without it ever coming back on him. If I was shanked while behind bars, no one would ever look in his direction.

Tears fill my eyes, my situation becoming increasingly hopeless. To think, there were moments I was upset on the island. Even being chained, naked, in the bunker was far better than this. I'd happily switch positions now, would take the bunker gladly. At least there I had the promise of good sex ahead of me. I realize just how different it felt to be with any of the guys—even Brody—compared to this. I'd wanted them, had lusted over them. I'd never been repulsed in the way I am with Don.

"Then just you take me," I try. "I'm not resisting arrest. I'll come with you happily, just not with him. Please." I'm pleading with him, holding his eye contact, trying to get him to see how genuine I am.

Edwardo frowns. "Why?"

"Because he killed my mother, and that's why I ran. I knew he'd find me and do whatever it took to keep me quiet."

"Don wouldn't do something like that," he scoffs.

"He pushed her down the stairs, and then he hit her in the head with a golf club."

"How could you know that?"

"I saw him washing off the club while she was lying bleeding at the bottom of the stairs. Who would do that? He'd already called the ambulance and the police, saying that he found her, and that it was an accident, but while he was waiting, he cleaned off the item he used to kill her."

"Bullshit."

I carry on. "When the police arrived, I tried to tell them what had happened, but they were all like you—on his side. They were all his cop buddies, and he was weeping and wailing over her body, and no one was listening to me. They called me hysterical—like I didn't have a reason to be. My mother was dead, and my stepfather had killed her."

"Why would he do that?"

I give a cold laugh. "Because he'd gotten bored of her. Because he had his sights on someone different."

Edwardo fixes me with his brown eyes. "Who?"

"Me. I had no choice but to leave. He knew that I knew, and he was willing to destroy me. That's why he's come after me now. It's got nothing to do with any bogus drug charge. It's because he wants to see the end of me."

I can tell I'm getting through to him. His eyes are more focused on me, and he's got a small furrow between his brow as he thinks.

"Look, just put me on the dinghy and take me to shore yourself and take me to a police station. I'll talk to whoever is listening. Just don't let him be the one who takes me."

I have no idea how much I can trust Edwardo. The fact he's working with Don doesn't bode well, but it isn't as though I'm overwhelmed with options. If Edwardo knows how bent Don is, then he won't care what I say because most likely, Edwardo is crooked, too. But if Edwardo is a good guy who already has his doubts about Don, he might just believe me.

"How can I be sure this isn't just a trick to escape?" Edwardo says.

I jangle my cuffed wrists. "What do you think I'm going to be able to do with my hands cuffed behind my back? Besides, you're armed, aren't you? Men like you never go anywhere without a gun."

He purses his lips and lifts the bottom of his white linen shirt to reveal the handgun tucked into the waistband of his pants. I suck in a breath, though it's no more than I'd already suspected.

"So, I'm right. What can I possibly do to escape when I'm cuffed and you're armed?"

He bites his lower lip, and glances over his shoulder toward where Don is.

"He's distracted, focused on driving the boat. If we're going to do it, we need to do it now. I'm not asking you to let me go. Take me on shore and straight to the nearest police station. Just do it without him."

"Okay," Edwardo says.

I almost burst into tears with relief. "Thank you. Thank you so much."

"But we move quickly and quietly, and we go now."

I'm not going to argue with that.

He takes me by my upper arm and helps me to my feet. My heart races, my breath short and tight in my chest. I'm fully aware this is the only chance I'll get to escape. I don't even care if I'm just going to end up in a police station—being away from Don is worth whatever comes next. If these drug charges are real, I'll have to figure out a way to hire a fucking good lawyer to prove them wrong.

The thought of needing a lawyer—a *good* lawyer, not some useless piece of crap the court issues—immediately makes me think of money. I was so close to getting that million bucks, but it's all ruined now. Even if I managed to speak to Rafferty and explain what had happened, I still broke the contract by leaving. It might not have been willingly, but I still left the island.

Don is sitting at the wheel, facing away from us. He's focused on the water and, I'm assuming, not hitting anything. It's dark now, and I hope the gloom will help shelter us from view. The dinghy is attached to the side of the boat. It isn't going to be easy to lower it into the water and make a jump for it, but what choice do we have?

An image pops into my mind—that of me grabbing Edwardo's gun and shooting Don in the back of the head. I imagine Don slumping forward, his body over the wheel, blood dripping onto the floor of the cabin. It would be quick and easy, and I'd never have to worry about my stepfather again.

I'd be free.

But there's no way I'll get Edwardo's weapon from him and, even if I somehow got my hands uncuffed and tried it, thing wouldn't end well for me. For one, Don would hear the tussle for the gun, and for two, I'd then have Edwardo to deal with. I might not be a drug dealer, as Don claims, but, if I shot Don, I would be a murderer.

Edwardo jerks his head toward the side of the boat. With my arms cuffed, I'm useless. I can't do anything but watch as he unhooks the rope tethering the dinghy. If this doesn't work, and I end up in the water, there's a good chance I'll drown. I might be able to tread water for a short while, maybe lie on my back and float, but without the use of my arms, I won't be able to swim properly, and I doubt I'll last long.

A cooling saltwater spray hits my face, and I know—if I live long enough—it will leave white tracks over my skin.

We bump and bounce across the waves. In the distance, the first specks of light appear. We're approaching the mainland farther down the coast, though it's still some distance away. The island and the resort have long since vanished from view.

My heart hurts. Before now, when I'd thought of dying, my main regret was that I'd never made Don pay for what he did. Now, however, I discover a new regret. I'll never get to find out what might have become of all of us. I didn't think I was imagining it when I felt something growing between us all. Maybe Brody was the one to kick back against it, but his reaction was only because he'd felt it, too. It scared him, and he reacted. Were the others blaming him now? I hoped not. This wasn't Brody's fault. Brody might have been the reason I'd ended up alone, but ultimately Don is the reason I'm gone.

It occurs to me that Don is also the reason I met the four of them. If I hadn't been running and hiding, I never would have gone for that job at *The Limit*. And if I hadn't needed the money so badly to start a new life for myself, and hopefully hire an investigator to put Don behind bars, I never would have stayed. I'd have heard their terms and been out of there quicker than a rat up a drainpipe.

In some strange way, do I have something to thank Don for?

Maybe, but there's no way in hell I'm thanking the sick fuck for anything.

One end of the dinghy drops and hits the water. I suck in a breath and hold it, my entire body poised for the shout of 'stop' that I'm certain will come from the wheelhouse. Edwardo freezes, too, and glances over at me. I meet his eye and swallow, hard.

But nothing happens, and with a quick nod, he turns back to the job at hand to work on releasing the other side of the boat.

It drops into the water. Only a loose line prevents it from floating away.

Edwardo puts his hand out to me and beckons me forward with a curl of his fingers. It isn't going to be easy climbing down with no hands. I want to ask him to uncuff me, but I don't know if his keys would even work on these cuffs, and there's no way we're going to ask Don to do it.

He reaches for me, clearly seeing that I'm going to need help—

The crack of a gunshot shatters the air, and I scream. I expect to feel pain, to stumble forward, to glance down and see blood...

But I'm not the one who's been shot.

Edwardo drops his chin and lifts one shaking hand to touch the circle of red blooming on his chest.

I stare, horrified, as he tilts backward, as though in slow motion, and falls from the boat. He half hits the dinghy and bounces like a ragdoll, and then strikes the water.

"Edwardo!" I scream.

He has a split second to raise his arm to me before he vanishes beneath the surface. I let out a sob. This is my fault. If I hadn't persuaded him to take me in the dinghy, he would be alive right now.

A strange kind of silence falls over the boat. I know Don is behind me, that he's holding a gun—most likely pointed at my back—and that he's more than willing to kill. I briefly debate throwing myself overboard. If my hands weren't cuffed behind my back, I'd be in the water already. Would I rather take my chances with the water than risk a bullet in my back? But, deep down, I know Don will only shoot me if he absolutely has to. At least until he's done what he wants with me and has had enough.

Slowly, I turn around.

He's just as I've pictured, standing in a wide-legged stance, his gun—which I assume is police-issued—aimed directly at me. His square jaw is clenched, his eyes sparking with fury.

"Well, that was fucking stupid, wasn't it, Honor?"

I don't even dare speak.

He stalks over to me and grabs my arm and drags me inside the cabin. He reaches into his pocket and takes out the keys to the cuffs. For one crazy moment, I think he's going to set me free. He undoes one of the cuffs but keeps a viselike grip on my arm, preventing me from lashing out at him. Then he hooks the chain of the cuff over one of the bars attached to the wall of the boat—something put there for support during rough seas. He clips the cuff back around my wrist, so I'm now attached to the boat, but he doesn't move back and continues to lean right into me.

His large body engulfs my personal space, and the heat of his breath gusts across the top of my head. I press myself into the metal bar behind me, trying to create room.

Any chance of escape has vanished.

"What the fuck do you want with me?"

"To make sure you keep your mouth shut."

"I already have, haven't I? I've not said a word to anyone." Apart from Rafferty and the others, but it's not as though I've told them everything.

"And how long is that likely to last? You'll spill it all eventually."

There's no point in trying to plead ignorance. We both know I saw him that day.

His hand brushes my breast, and I freeze.

He notices and chuckles. "I always knew you had a thing for me, back when your mother was still alive. You were forever prancing around half naked, showing your ass off to me. I used to feel so sorry for your poor mom."

The way he's twisted that scenario in his head sends fresh anger and frustration through me.

"What the fuck are you talking about? I never did that."

"Always leaving the bathroom door unlocked, and open a crack, tempting me to take a peek. God, that young, firm flesh, all damp and pink out of the shower. I've got to say that I got myself off on that a good few times."

"I never left the door open! You just used to barge in, knowing I was right out of the shower."

"You know, I would have killed you already, but frankly, I'm being selfish. I've waited so long to get a taste of your sweet little pussy that I want to take my time with you. How old are you now?"

"Why?"

He takes a guess. "Twenty? Twenty-one? Hmm. Might be too old for most of their liking, but I'm sure some of them will enjoy a sweet bit of virgin pussy."

I have no idea who he's talking about, but I laugh out loud. "I'm not a virgin. You think I've been saving myself? Well, I haven't. I've been fucking anyone who looks my way. I've had more men inside me than a bar at happy hour."

Fury crosses his features, but I'd rather have him angry with me than lusting over me. This could go one of two ways. Either he thinks I'm used material and doesn't want to touch me, or he decides that if everyone has fucked me already, then he might as well do the same.

I'm betting on it being the idea of me as some innocent little virgin, his wife's young daughter, the forbidden fruit, that had gotten him all hot and bothered. If I'm right—for the moment, anyway—he might leave me alone. There's a chance he'll get over it soon enough, though, and take what he wants.

He also might decide that if I'm damaged goods now, he might as well kill me already.

I can only wait, terrified, to see how this will go down.

Chapter Four
Wilder

THOUGH IT'S THE MIDDLE of the night, none of us even tries to sleep. How can we when Honor is still missing and potentially in the hands of her stepfather? I wish I'd paid more attention to her when she'd been here. I wish I'd asked her more questions about her life and her background and the person she was running from. I can't help but be furious with myself, and with the others, too, that we didn't care more. She'd tried to tell us, but we didn't listen.

I cannot get the name of that boat out of my mind. There's no way it can be a coincidence. Pastor Wren used to say that specific phrase repeatedly during his sermons, and also during his private time with his special boys, as he called us.

It makes no sense, though. How can Honor's stepfather be linked to Pastor Wren in any way?

Every now and then, my eyes grow heavy and I slip into an almost dreamlike state, only to startle awake again as more thoughts hit me. My mind is racing, trying to make connections and maps between a corrupt LA cop and a pastor who has spent most of his life on the move, a never-ending quest not to be caught for his crimes.

Something occurs to me and sends my heart racing.

There's one thing Pastor Wren does have a lot of...money.

If there's one thing corrupt cops like, it's cold, hard cash. What if at some point Pastor Wren needed a California cop in his pocket? He could easily have looked into which police officers would possibly be amenable to bribes, and maybe through doing that he found Honor's stepfather.

Maybe I'm putting too much weight into the name of the boat, but I can't seem to shake it. Besides, it makes sense, doesn't it? Men like them are drawn together like magnets.

We have a private investigator on the mainland who has been charged with tracking down Wren. Only recently did he report that Wren was using an alias and preaching at a church in Reno. The chances of Honor's stepfather taking her there are slim but not none. But I'm wary of sending us all racing off on a wild goose chase only to miss clues about where her stepfather actually may have taken her.

I'd left the others for a short time, needing a break from the intensity in that room. Now, I need to get back to them.

We need Asher on this to do some digging. Pastor Wren hides his tracks far too well. We've been after the man for the longest time. Don, however, might not be quite so savvy.

I've met a lot of cops in my time, and the ones who tend to be corrupt also tend to be overconfident. They think having the weight of the law behind them gives them a power to do anything they want. It's often that false belief in their own God-like ability to handle anything that comes their way that proves their ultimate downfall.

From what Honor told us, and from what we've found out ourselves, I would bet good money on Don being one of those overly confident, arrogant assholes who has left a trail of breadcrumbs for anyone technically competent enough to follow. You don't get much more technically competent than Asher.

Despite my exhaustion from the lack of sleep, there's an energy buzzing within me as I think we might have a way to find Honor and the pastor, and Don gave it to us. I head to the kitchen, and, after pouring myself a cup of black coffee from the pot on the side, I walk into the office.

I open the door and pause. Sitting in one of the chairs typing away furiously is Asher.

"I was about to call you," I tell him.

"Oh, yeah," he says, without stopping what he's doing or glancing at me.

"Yes. I haven't been able to get the coincidence of that boat's name out of my mind."

Asher folds his lips into a thin line. "I've been the same. It has to be more than a coincidence."

"When was the last time we heard from the private investigator on the mainland? Do we know if Wren is still in Reno?"

"I'm not sure. We've all been a little...distracted...with Honor around."

The weight of something that feels a lot like guilt settles in the room. We should have moved sooner on the information that had been fed to us. We'd always been so laser focused before on finding Wren and making him pay, but Honor had given us something else to fixate upon. Maybe that hadn't been a bad thing. A life that was purely about revenge wasn't one being lived at all.

"We need to make contact with him," I say, "find out if anything has changed with Wren."

Asher raises an eyebrow. "You think Wren might know where Honor is? It feels like you're grasping to me."

I shrug. "Maybe I am, but it's not like we're drowning in leads. The PI might be able to look into things from Wren's side, see if he can find a connection to Don or Honor. You could check from Don's end of the equation."

"Already on it," Asher says.

I sip at the dark, strong coffee as I watch his fingers fly over the keyboard. He uses that machine the way an award-winning musician can play a piano or a guitar. At times, it's as if the keyboard and the screen in front of him become a part of him.

"I've already found something interesting," Asher says. "It seems Don managed to buy himself that boat outright. It cost one-point-two million dollars. You want to tell me where a cop gets that kind of money?"

He finally stops typing and turns to look at me.

I can see in his intelligent eyes, the thoughts that I'm having are running through his mind, too.

"You think the pastor gave him the money to buy it?"

Asher shrugs. "If he did, Don might even have asked our esteemed pastor if he could name the boat after him. Wren wouldn't want that, but he might have given Don his favorite saying. Can you imagine the ego boost for the pastor, knowing that a corrupt cop went and named a boat after him in gratitude?"

For a long time, I've been convinced that Pastor Wren is one of the most dangerous kinds of predators out there. He's not a sociopath. No, he's something far worse. Wren is a full-blown malignant narcissist. He gaslights, and lies, and manipulates, and through it all he revels in the adoration of the crowds he gathers around him as he preaches. He's cunning and manipulative, but he also has a weakness, and that weaknesses is that he can't control his sick desires. However, neither can he control his need for adulation.

I truly believe someone more sociopathic, without the emotional pull that Wren feels whenever he receives attention and praise, wouldn't have run the risk of carrying out their crimes while at the same time pursuing local levels of fame as a preacher of God.

Due to my experiences as a child, I've read a lot about people with dangerous personalities, and a lot of experts say that malignant narcissists are the worst of all. I don't know Honor's stepfather, but from the little I've heard, he strikes me as the more common grandiose type of narcissist. A little bit flashy. Very much overconfident. Bothered about how he looks, of course, and a cheating piece of crap who can't keep it in his pants.

If he got entangled with the pastor, he will definitely be the junior partner. I despise Wren, but I also respect his deviousness and his ability to commit evil. To not do so would be dangerous.

The sense of impending doom I've been feeling ever since making the connection only grows stronger.

"If there is a link between them," I say, "it means our girl is in much more danger than we originally thought."

"She *is* our girl, too, isn't she?" Asher states the question with a sort of melancholy sadness behind the words.

I don't know why he frames it is a question, because we both know it's the truth. Rafferty does, too, and even Brody, despite his actions, knows she belongs with us.

We've never been in this situation before, but if I know one thing about us, it is that anybody does us wrong, we'll get our revenge. It might take us a long time, the way it has with the pastor, but we will get it in the end. You take what's ours, and we come for it.

"Yes, she is our girl, and we need to get our girl back," I say.

"Absolutely." Asher glances back at the screen. "How the hell are we supposed to figure out where she's been taken, though?"

"I thought that was your skillset."

He blows out a frustrated breath and shakes his head. "I've got to tell you, man, I'm hitting a dead end here."

I pace as I sip my coffee. I ought to eat something, but my stomach is too queasy to be able to contemplate facing food right now. I turn suddenly to Asher. "Maybe we're looking at this the wrong way," I say.

"What do you mean?"

"Only, we're looking for a clue as to which direction Don took our girl. Perhaps we should start looking at the other end, the destination."

Asher narrows his eyes and looks at me as if I've grown a second head. "Great plan, Wilder. The trouble is we don't know their destination, so how do we go looking for something we don't know?"

I grin at him as the idea solidifies in my mind. "That boat can't carry that much fuel, right? I mean, the hold can't be that big. It's not safe to have gallons and gallons of that stuff sloshing around. Presuming he must have a limited amount of fuel, there aren't that many places he could reach. So, we start by looking at the places he might land."

Asher slaps his hand against his thigh as if in frustration with his own flesh. "Are you kidding me with this, Wilder? There are absolutely tons of places he could land that craft. He doesn't have to go to a registered marina. He could simply pull up to anywhere along the shore."

"I still say it's worth a try. We contact all the small marinas and the places where he could dock for a few nights and ask if a boat with the name *Secret Truth* has landed. We can also try to gain access to the footage of any cameras along the opposite coast. Surely you can do that?"

"I can do it, but it's like looking for a needle in a haystack. But you might actually be onto something with the idea of starting to look at the other end."

I cock my head to one side and observe him.

"Maybe we ought to be looking for the registration on Don's car. I don't know...any rentals that have taken place in his name. Or any alias he uses. I've been spending so many hours looking at footage trying to figure out where the boat could have gone, and instead my time might be better spent trying to figure out where the hell Don is hiding out."

I'm feeling useless in my inability to help Asher in his search, and it's making me bad tempered. "I just want that piece of shit found and dealt with."

"I get it, big guy. So do I. You know, there's one thing that can buy almost anything, and that includes information."

"Oh? And what's that, great sage?"

"Limitless wealth. Limitless wealth can buy most people and things. Everyone has a price. And we have a lot of wealth."

He's not wrong on the first part but is entirely incorrect on the second. *We* don't have that.

"I can see what you're thinking," he says. "Rafferty is going to be in on this. Don't you worry. He's going to be all the way in with us, wanting to find our girl. He feels the same way we do. The only one who doesn't is Brody."

"So, what are you saying? We should throw Rafferty's millions at this to try to solve the issue that way?"

Asher stands and stretches his arms, shaking them out as he steps away from the computer. "Think about it. A corrupt cop like Don, he's gonna have made a lot of enemies. There will be people who work in his department who can't stand the man. Hell, he might have friends, but I bet you anything even they can be purchased for the right price. That's the thing about corrupt people, they like to hang out with other corrupt people. We must ask a lot of questions and throw money at it if needs be, and we will soon be able to find out what cars he owns, other than his main one, and where he likes to go on his boat, and if there is a part of the coast he particularly loves. We need to send someone down to his precinct to start digging around among his friends."

"That could be a rather dangerous thing to do," I point out. "So, I'll do it."

"Nah, we're going to need you here. Your strength is going to be crucial if we come up against Don and some of his men in a fight. If anyone goes, it should either be Brody, because he's a fucking dick that caused all this in the first place, or me."

"Why you?"

"Well, first, because of my boyish charm." He grins at me and snaps his teeth.

I can't help but laugh, despite the anxiety gnawing away at my insides.

"Second, though, it makes sense. I can take my laptop and phone with me, so any information I get, I can use to do more digging computer-wise on the spot. You might get information, but then what would you do with it? You'd need to relay it to me, anyway."

I don't like it. We don't split up. Ever. It's not safe for us to with the pastor out there, always on the lookout for anyone from his past who might do him harm. We shouldn't even be alive, never mind searching for the man. What Asher is suggesting is fundamentally dangerous, for him more than us.

"We need to speak to Rafferty first," I say.

"Speak to me about what?"

I slam my hand over my heart. "Jesus Christ," I exclaim. "You are one sneaky motherfucker. I didn't even hear you come into the room. How long have you been standing there?"

"Long enough to hear Asher is suggesting running off and doing something possibly suicidal."

Asher goes up to Rafferty and stands right in front of him. "It makes sense, and you know it does. We have our rules about not going anywhere on our own, but we can't only think of ourselves now. We need to put *her* first. If you don't let me, I'll just go anyway. It makes sense for me to do this and for you three to stay here so you can get to her as quickly as possible when I find the information. We've always been about the revenge and nothing else. It's why we always said we'd stick together and never risk one of us getting harmed. We needed our revenge more than anything else. Now, though, there's something more important to us. I know I'm not alone in feeling that way. If I get hurt, so be it. If it means we can save Honor, then it's worth trying. Like I say, I'm going either way, but I'd rather go with your support and blessing."

He pushes past Rafferty and stalks out of the room. When he leaves, it's as if he's taken half the air in the room with him. As if somehow, he sucked some of the energy right out of the vortex we are left standing in.

"Christ, I think he's got it the worst out of all of us," Rafferty grouses.

"Oh, I don't know, I think I've got it pretty bad, too," I say with a deep, but short laugh. "What he says is correct, though," I point out. "One of us needs to go and do some digging on the ground. We need some of your money, and some of Asher's smarts, and we might luck out and find out where Don could be holding our girl. Once we do, we can go and get her back."

"What if we're too late? What if he takes her and kills her right away?" Rafferty is normally so controlled, but now his cool blue eyes fill with emotion, and pain turns them a deeper hue than usual.

"He's not going to kill her," I say. "At least not yet.

"How can you be so sure?"

I sigh and glance at the floor before looking back to him to answer.

"Because if he wanted to do that, he could have murdered her in the cove and dumped her body in the waves. Then we'd have found her body already. He's taken a risk by snatching her and keeping her alive. He wants to take his time, and he wants to play with her."

I leave the awful truth hanging in the room behind me as I turn and follow Asher out of the door.

Chapter Five
Honor

SOME HOURS LATER, DON reaches whatever spot on the mainland he's been heading toward all this time and guides the boat toward shore.

I'm nauseated from the prolonged swell of the ocean, and I'm sure my face is an interesting shade of green. I hate throwing up, so I'm relieved I've managed to prevent myself from vomiting. If I had been sick, though, I'd have made sure it hit Don.

The boat bumps against the jetty, and Don vanishes from view as he does whatever he needs to do to prevent the boat from drifting away again. I try to get a view of where we are, but darkness swathes the land. The moon is a crescent cut out of the indigo sky, and the wave of bright dots of starlight don't do much to light the way. I strain my ears, hoping to catch the distant hum of cars on a road, or of voices, but there's only the slosh of water against the jetty and the rhythmic call of cicadas from somewhere onshore.

The heavy thud of footsteps signals Don's return, and then he's back, looming over me. He uses the key to unlock the cuffs, but my relief is only momentary as he unhooks the chain, and quickly snaps them shut again, so my hands are now cuffed in front of my body. He grabs me by the forearm, his fingers branding red marks into my skin. He ignores the way I stumble and shake as I trip behind him getting off the boat which continues to bob with the movement of the waves against the jetty. The man is insane.

He killed Edwardo.

Right in front of me, he simply pulled the trigger and killed that man. Another cop, too. The image of Edwardo's rounded eyes staring up at me, filled with pain and terror, the way his fingers reached for me, just as he sank beneath the dark surface of the water jumps into my mind. I squeeze my eyes shut, willing it away. Did Edwardo have family who will miss him? Will they ever get his body back to bury him, or will they live the rest of their lives frozen at the point where their loved one vanished without a trace?

Something else occurs to me.

Oh, God, Don killed another cop right in front of me, which means he doesn't care that I saw.

It means I'm probably next. Unless...I can give him a reason to keep me around. My heart sinks at the thought, but I know I need to keep myself alive until the men come for me.

I'm convinced my men will find me. I don't know where I've gained such a bone deep belief from, but it's as real as the air I'm breathing. Even Brody, I believe, will try to find me. Wilder and Asher, though, I think would burn the world to the ground to save me from this man. Between them, they have the skills and the smarts to do so. It means I owe it to them to keep myself alive until they do.

Even if that means playing Don's sick games.

Even if that means giving Don what he's always wanted.

My blood curdles at the very thought. The idea of his hands on me makes my stomach churn and my skin crawl. But I realize the possibility isn't affecting me in the same way it once did. I'm no longer terrified at the prospect.

Can I do it, though? Can I offer myself to a man I find so utterly vile in every way? Well, not *every* way. I hate the fact that I can see how handsome he is, but I can't deny it. I can't deny that as I've grown and blossomed into a woman who understands the pleasures of the flesh, I can see him for the prime example of a powerful male that he is. Physically, at least.

I don't desire him, because everything else about him is trash. His personality, his morals, and his behavior are all the lowest of the low.

To save my life, however? If I closed my eyes, I could simply let myself feel the hard planes of his body. Maybe then I can imagine he is Rafferty, or perhaps Brody. He's similar in build to those two, I suppose. Not as big as Wilder, but bulkier than Ash. Yeah, like Brody.

This may be a way I can get through it. Pretend he's someone else. Let myself feel some pleasure, despite how wrong it is.

If I don't, I have a horrible feeling he will grow bored quickly and get rid of me.

He likes to be worshipped and adored, but it's a tightrope you walk with someone like Don. He eventually gets bored of that and moves on to a new victim to give him a whole new sense of power from the way *they* hero worship him. In the beginning I do believe he uses the way women adore him in the same sense a cocaine addict uses the drug. It fills his veins with burning, thrumming energy and gives him power.

I saw it firsthand with my own mother. In the early days, you could imagine they were the most perfectly in love couple you'd ever seen. Of course, if you were behind closed doors with them the way I was, you could see quite easily that it was very one-sided. It was all about Don being the admired and adored God of our house, and my mother being the adoring and admiring little worshiper. He loved her playing that role at the beginning. I think for quite a while there were no other women. Hell, in the beginning, he didn't even turn his attentions on me. After a while, he grew bored of the easy supply of hero worship from Mom and decided to look for a new supply elsewhere.

The way he enjoyed her attentions at the start means I have a window where I can keep him on the hook before he grows bored and looks for someone fresh and new.

I must believe that within this time frame my men will find me.

The wind whips at my hair, and I shiver. It's dark where Don landed the boat, and I keep tripping on stones and rocks as he drags me down the small jetty and onto a beach, overshadowed by great big cliffs. Dawn's early light isn't reaching us yet, but I pray it'll be here soon. Hours have passed since I was taken on the boat, but I've lost track as to how many. My legs don't yet feel solid beneath me, and I swear I can still feel the rise and fall of the boat, as though I'm somehow carrying the memory of it in my muscles.

My hope that he might be forced to dock the boat somewhere there are other people quickly fades. He wouldn't want us to be picked up by any cameras operating the coastal roads or marinas, where most boats dock. This way, there are no witnesses to our arrival.

I'm not sure how he intends to get us off this beach because I can't see a path out, and there is no way we can climb these cliffs. Still pulling me roughly behind him, Don increases his speed, and I stumble to the ground, crying out as my knees scrape against shingle and rock.

"Get the hell up," he growls.

Yanking hard on the handcuffs, he pulls me to my feet and drags me forward once more. After a few more moments of this, he stops suddenly, and my front slams into his back.

For a second or two, he lets go of me. The urge to run rides me hard, but I know there's nowhere for me to go. After all, the man has a gun, and my hands are cuffed, so escape is highly unlikely. I need to keep my wits about me and use my brains right now. Not do something crazy, like trying to escape when there is no chance of doing so.

Don bends down, and I realize he's rummaging in a dark bag that I can only just make out in the dim moonlight.

He takes out something long and black, and for a second, I panic that he's going to hit me with it. Instead, he clicks a button and a blinding beam of light flashes in front of my eyes before he moves it away and points it down the beach. It's a flashlight, and I breathe out in relief that it's not something to bludgeon me to death with. Although I'm sure he could use it for that purpose too. Don is nothing if not resourceful when it comes to his violence.

"Come on," he says gruffly as he starts moving again. "If you keep up, I won't drag you behind me, but you lag or try to run, I'll beat you so hard with this flashlight you won't see anything for a week. And I will simply drag you behind me by your ankles if I must."

I'm under no illusions whatsoever that these are idle threats. Don is more than capable of carrying out his warnings and hurting me.

As we near the far side of the small bay and reach one of the cliffs, I realize there is what appears to be an entrance to a cave. Oh, my God, no. Instinctively, I stop.

I can't go in there. Memories of the cave back at the island and what happened while I was in there flash into my head. While I enjoyed being with the guys, going through the same thing with Don fills me with such existential dread that I think I would rather Don beat me to death with a flashlight.

"What the hell is your problem?" Don turns to me, grabs hold of the handcuffs, and pulls me forward again.

"I don't want to go into that cave," I tell him.

"It's not a cave," he says. "It looks like one from the outside, but once you get in there, and you turn left, it's basically an extremely steep and high ravine cut into the cliffs. It leads through a narrow path to the beach at the other side. Once we get there, I have a rental car waiting for us."

"Where are you taking me?" I demand.

"Somewhere we can have a good chat," he says with a heavy dose of sarcasm.

I hate him so much I want to take hold of the flashlight and smash him so hard on the head his skull cracks like the shell of an egg and his brains spill out like messy yolk.

Somewhat shocked at myself for the ferocity of my thoughts, I try to clear my head and think about what he said.

A place for us to talk. Right. But it gives me chance to take control, and to be the one in the driver's seat here. For a while, at least. Buying myself time until I can get out of this mess.

"Will I be able to take a shower and change?" I ask.

He stops walking and slowly swivels his head until he faces me.

I know I'm playing a dangerous game right now, but for the first time in a long while, I feel as if I have something worth surviving for. I think, slowly but surely, I've somehow managed to fall in love with my four strange and brooding employers on the island. I want to see where this thing between us could go. And I also want my damn money. I earned it. More than anything, though, I want this man dead. And I know the four men who hired me to be their plaything can bring about his demise.

All I need to do is play for time.

Mentioning showers to Don is like a red cape to a bull. Or perhaps, one might more aptly say, it's a tantalizing glimpse of stocking to a leg man who hasn't had sex in years. Don liked nothing more than sneaking in the bathroom when I was in there, and me asking about a shower is about as innocent as the things I've been doing on the island.

It makes me realize something profound; I've come a very long way since my first days thinking I was a maid. At first, I'd been afraid of the things those men wanted me to do, and then intrigued, and in time enticed by them. I grew in my confidence, and in my belief in myself now both as a sexual being but also as a strong woman. I ran for hours in the heat. I fought hard. And through it all, despite at times what seemed to be their best attempts to take it from me, I kept my dignity.

If Don thinks someone as sleazy and pathetic as himself now gets to take it away, he's very wrong.

I don't see sex as something scary anymore, and I'm not afraid to use my body if it gets me what I want.

"Yes, there are showers in the house," he says slowly as if trying to figure out whether I meant anything by my question.

"Good to know, because I'm a very dirty girl."

There. Tease dropped.

The light is still dim, but I can see enough to understand that he hasn't figured this out. I like that. I like the sense of power it gives me in this moment. He's the predator, but maybe, just maybe, I can turn him into the prey.

He yanks on the cuffs and pulls me into the crevasse. Instantly, my surroundings change. The temperature plummets. The moonlight vanishes. Even the acoustics change, and the crash of the ocean on the beach is replaced by our heavy breathing and the crunch of our footsteps. I'm forced to duck to avoid cracking my head on the rock ceiling.

Don uses the flashlight to guide his own way, and I have no choice but to follow in his footsteps. By the time my feet land where his were, the illumination has long since moved on, and I have to trust my memory.

It feels like we're inside the cave-tunnel for far longer than we are, but finally we emerge into the fresh air.

With relief, I straighten and suck in a lungful of oxygen. I can still hear the sea, and there's a brackish tang to the air. I blink, my eyes adjusting to the change in light.

We're on another beach now. A car sits at the far end, where sand and shingle turn to scrubby grass. Don marches us to it, opens the passenger door of the generic, silver car. He pushes me into the seat before slamming the door closed on me. I can't fasten my seatbelt because I still have the handcuffs on, but when Don gets into the driver's side he leans over and pulls it around me. His hand brushes my breast, and he pauses, deliberately meeting my eye. I hold his, refusing to back down or give in to the tears that have been permanently lodged in the back of my throat since my realization that he found me. A small smile touches the corner of his lips, and he continues to pull the strap down, clicking it into place.

He does his own belt and starts the car, driving off the scrub land and onto the road.

We drive in silence, and as we pass under the lights at the side of the small country road we are on, I think about the ways I could seduce this man. I need to do it in a clever manner. If I give him too much at once, he'll get bored too quickly. If I don't tease him enough, he's either going to force me into giving him what he wants or get bored for the exact opposite reason of him getting it too easily. This is going to be a delicate balancing act, but I do believe it is one I can pull off. This man was so terrifying to me before, but now that I've faced four huge, insatiable, and, at times, angry men, he doesn't hold the same power over me.

Thirty minutes pass, and we approach the driveaway of a property, in the middle of nowhere, of course. He unclips my seatbelt, opens the driver's door, gets out, and walks around to my side. He opens my door and hauls me out of the car.

"What is this place?" I ask.

"Just a rental," he says. "It's got all the luxuries a girl like you might need, though."

He flashes me what he probably thinks is a panty-melting grin.

We reach the house, and he opens the door and ushers me inside. When the door closes behind me, he drives home bolts on both the top and bottom. Then he takes a small key from his pocket before unfastening my cuffs.

I rub my wrists, frowning at the red lines marring the skin.

"I really don't want to hurt you, Honor," he says. "But you try anything, and I'll beat you so hard, you will wish you were dead. I know how to do it without breaking any bones but while putting you in so much pain you can't bear it."

"Wow, you really *do* sound like a guy who doesn't want to hurt me." For a moment, I forget my seduction plan and let the sneer show on my face.

The slap, when it comes, is a shock.

"Christ, I've always hated that smart mouth of yours," he snarls, shaking his hand out after hitting me.

My cheek stings, but he must have tempered the blow because it doesn't hurt all that much. I need to get myself under control and stop annoying him. Not because I really care whether he's angry at me, but because every time I make him rage, there's the risk he'll lose ultimate control and do something to harm me before my men find me.

My men. I let that sink in as it rolls around luxuriously in my mind, offering me a comfort in the stark reality of my situation.

They're coming for me. I know it to be true. And the knowledge gives me power. All I must do is harness that power and bide my time.

I imagine Don's expression as he comes face-to-face with Rafferty, Wilder, Brody, and Asher. There's no way he won't be intimidated by the four of them. One thing worries me, however, and that's the gun. If any of them were to get shot while trying to take Don down, I'd never forgive myself.

I look up at my stepfather through my lashes, and as innocently as I can muster, I say, "Please, may I have a shower? I'm cold and wet."

He angles his head before replying. "Of course, you may."

He takes my hand in his and leads me up the stairs. I try not to recoil from the feeling of his fingers around mine.

On the second-floor landing, he throws open a door and, in front of me, is what I would have thought of as a magnificent bathroom in the past, before my time on the island. Now I've seen luxury beyond compare.

"You can shower in here. There is everything you need: shampoo, conditioner, body wash, perfume." His gaze takes on an intense and unnerving focus as a small smile lifts one side of his mouth. "I purchased all the things I could think a beautiful girl like you might need."

The way he's looking at me makes me think I might have gotten this all wrong. Maybe this isn't simply a game to him.

There's an almost lovesick sheen to his gaze, and he's staring at me as if I've hung the stars in the night sky. Oh, God, does Don...does he somehow, in a sick way, love me?

Perhaps there's more to his deranged desires than simple narcissistic greed. Maybe, in a truly sick and twisted way, Don really is obsessed with me. That only means I must be even more careful with this strange game we're starting to play with one another.

If this is way more than just an ego boost for him, and another notch on his belt, then the timing is even more crucial. Take this too slow, and I risk angering him beyond all belief. Frustrating him until he snaps. Take it too quickly, however, and I risk igniting his suspicions and mistrust. If only I could somehow know for sure exactly what kind of an enemy I'm facing. As it is, however, I will need to use all my wits, and all my charms, to stay ahead of whatever it is that Don has planned for me.

"Thank you, *Daddy*," I say.

The word gives me the creeps when I say it to Don like that, but it's a way for me to test a theory.

A new and disturbing theory.

As soon as I say the word, I realize I'm right.

His eyes widen, his nostrils flare, and his pupils darken. It seems Don doesn't simply have an interest in me as a trophy, but rather a full-blown and sick obsession with a girl who was his stepdaughter.

"Do you mind if I have some privacy now?" I ask with as much respect as I can put into my tone.

His voice is gruff, as if he's pouring it over gravel and rocks. "Take your time."

I can't help but glance down, and when I see the powerful bulge in his trousers, I get a strange and sick thrill.

This is so twisted and fucked up, but in a weird way, this is me taking my power and control because I'm not going to let him do one thing to me...because *I'm* going to be the one doing it to *him*.

I'm going to do whatever it takes to ensure he keeps me alive, and the moment I either get the chance to do it, or my men find me, then Don is dead.

Chapter Six
Brody

THOUGH THE OTHERS DON'T seem to be blaming me for what's happened, I can't help but blame myself. My stomach is a constant knot. My shame is a sickness lodged in the back of my throat. I've never regretted anything the way I regret my actions with Honor.

I can see now that I was wrong. Honor leaving wouldn't have brought the four of us closer together. If anything, the opposite would have happened. The others would have retreated into themselves, mourning her rejection, questioning why she'd left.

I get on the phone, and a male voice, thick with sleep, answers.

"Do you know what time it is?"

"I don't give a fuck," I say. "This is important."

There's a shuffle of sheets as the private investigator who works for us sits up in bed. I picture him flicking on the bedside lamp, and his wife or girlfriend shooting him an irritated look for disturbing his sleep.

Harris Carter.

We pay him enough to be on call twenty-four hours a day, seven days a week.

Carter grunts. "What's going on?"

"Is Wren still in Reno?" I ask.

"As I told Rafferty, it was just a *lead* on Wren being in Reno. If it's him, he's using a different name. I never had final confirmation."

"Why not?" I snap.

"I left the ball in your court. I fed that information back to you. It was up to the four of you to take the next actions. I've been waiting to hear from you about how you wanted to proceed."

"Well, you can take this as us notifying you. We think Wren might be connected to a man who has taken a woman we—" I interrupt myself.

I'd been about to say 'a woman we love.' The realization hits me like a punch to the chest. *Love?* What do any of us know about love? Are we even capable of such a thing?

I clear my throat and try again. "A woman who is important to us. The man's name is Don Bowen, and he's a detective with the LAPD. We have reason to believe he brought a boat called *Secret Truth* to the island and snatched Honor Armitage, though she may also be going under the name Honor Harper."

"What does this have to do with Wren?" Carter asks.

That familiar sense of shame sweeps over me, as it does any time I'm forced to think back to those days when I was just a boy and under the control of Pastor Wren. I hate talking about it. I'd prefer to stick my head in the sand and forget it ever happened, but such a thing is impossible. I am who

I am because of Wren. The things he did to me changed me irrevocably. There's an argument in science about nature versus nurture—if we are who we are more because of our genetics or more due to the outside influences of our family and home and surroundings. I feel like I was fucked over on both accounts. I never knew who my father was, and my mother was too weak—mentally and physically—to stand up to the likes of Pastor Wren. All she ever wanted was to please him, perhaps thinking, in some warped way, that giving him what he wanted would somehow get her a direct route to Heaven when her time came. I prefer to think anyone involved with him was sent down instead of up.

I was seventeen when I applied to join the army. It was the youngest age allowed, though I would have joined up years earlier, if they'd taken me. It was my way of escaping. Pastor Wren had been long gone by that point—moved on to torture his next victim, though it wasn't until years later that I'd learned one of those victims was Asher—but I'd needed to escape the small town where I'd grown up, and the mother who'd handed me over to a monster. I guess I'd hoped to escape myself as well. I'd been so filled with fury all the time, and I hadn't known what to do with it. I'd thought going into a career where I'd be paid to fight would give me an outlet, but it hadn't worked like that. It hadn't been an outlet. If anything, the opposite had happened, and I'd sucked up the violence surrounding me like a sponge.

It wasn't until Asher made contact with me through a snail mail letter that I'd understood what I needed to do.

Then I'd met my brothers and I'd been introduced to the island that had become my home.

Realizing I've left Carter hanging, I force my thoughts back to the present. "The name of the boat. It's something Wren used to say to us all. The secret truth. It's what he called his private 'sermons' with us."

It had been Wren's way of keeping us quiet. We were sworn to keep what happened during his times with us a secret, while he told us that the things he said and did to us were the one and only truth. God's truth. Of course, as we were so young, we believed Wren told us the truth, too. It was a sin to lie, or so he said.

A pause on the end of the line tells me Carter is considering what I've told him. Finally, he speaks. "You believe this Don Bowen is connected to Pastor Wren somehow?"

"Not just me," I say. "All four of us do. It's not just a coincidence. It can't be."

"What could be connecting them?"

I grind my molars. Finding out this stuff is *his* job. But then I remind myself that anything I can give him will only put him ahead in his investigations.

"We're just guessing right now, but we know Don is corrupt and Wren has plenty of money. It's possible Wren had Don in his pocket to help cover his tracks. We're going to make some inquiries on our end, but since you were already looking into Wren, we need you to find out how he's connected to Don. If Wren gave Don enough money to buy a fucking boat, and Don allowed Wren to name it, the two must be tight."

My head swims with the madness of Honor's stepfather being connected to the man who tormented all our childhoods.

BROKEN LIMITS 61

A different kind of thought suddenly occurs to me. What if it *isn't* a coincidence? What if Honor was directed to this job on the island intentionally to get to us? Would such a thing be possible?

I can't see how. Wren doesn't know the four of us have come together and set up *The Limit*. He probably still thinks of us as the little boys in his past and not the fully grown men we are now. Don wouldn't have had any clue that we're connected to Wren, either, and if he did, I highly doubt he'd send his virgin stepdaughter straight into our hands.

The whole situation is mind-bending. I don't like the way my thoughts grow tangled whenever I try to figure this mess out. It sets me on edge.

"Leave it with me," Carter says. "I'll get back to you."

"You understand this is highly time sensitive. There literally isn't a moment to waste."

"I understand."

I end the call and drop the phone to the desk, then put my head in my hands. What is happening to Honor right now? The best I can hope for is that she's curled up in bed somewhere—alone—hoping we're coming to find her. I pray that she knows we'll be coming for her, and that we wouldn't just abandon her. But what if her stepfather is hurting her? What if he's forcing himself on her? I've seen a photograph of this man. He isn't some sixty-year-old with a limp dick who has to take little blue pills to even get it up. He isn't much older than Rafferty and Wilder, and certainly wouldn't look out of place standing beside them.

The thought of his hands on Honor's pale skin, him fisting her long, dark hair, him forcing her legs apart and penetrating her mouth, her pussy, her ass with his fingers and cock while she fights beneath him makes me want to destroy the entire world to get to her. I've never experienced such intensity of emotion before, and I roar my pain, surprising even myself. How had I managed to fool myself into believing I didn't want her around? I'd tried to build a wall around my heart, but it had only ever been made from sand—easily washed away.

Something else occurs to me.

What if we get her back, and the things her stepfather has done to her have changed her permanently? She might be so traumatized by what she's been through that she can no longer stand us touching her.

A worse thought lingers in the back of my mind. I almost don't want to focus on it, probing at it like a sore tooth with my tongue, worried about what I might find. Will we see her differently if Don has fucked her? Before, she'd been our girl—only we'd touched her like that—but will we see her as damaged goods if she comes back to us? What if *we* are the ones who can't bring ourselves to touch *her*?

The possibility sickens me. What the fuck is wrong with my brain? If anyone is damaged goods, it's the four of us. I still remember the musky taste of Pastor Wren as he made me take to my knees and had me suck him as he recited prayers above my head.

However Honor comes back to us, we will give her whatever she needs. We'll comfort her and give her space and time—whatever it takes for her to heal. The four of us, of all people, know how it feels to have your autonomy taken away.

I force myself to my feet and go to the office to join the others.

"It's done," I tell them. "Harris Carter is back on the case."

Rafferty nods his approval. "Good. That's one step closer to finding Honor."

I hope he's right.

Asher clears his throat. "And I'll bring us another step closer by driving to Los Angeles to see what I can find out about Don."

Rafferty purses his lips. "You're not going alone."

"I'll go with you," Wilder offers.

Asher eyes him. "No offense, man, but no one is going to talk to me with you hanging around in the background."

That's the thing about Asher. He looks inconspicuous. Wilder, however, is the complete opposite.

"I'll go," I offer. "It's the least I can do."

Rafferty rubs his hand across his lips. "I don't like us splitting up."

"It won't be for long," Asher says. "And we're all big boys. I'm sure we can handle ourselves."

Rafferty nods. "Okay, but you stay in touch at all times. If you need to switch off your phone for any reason, you make sure you let the rest of us know first. I want everyone to have tracking set up on their phones as well, so we can easily find each other if something goes wrong."

Asher and I nod.

"What about Reno?" Wilder asks. "Should we go there?"

"It could be a wild goose chase," Rafferty says. "We don't know for sure yet that it was even definitely Wren the PI found there, and he may have moved on. We've got Carter back on it now, so I say we give him some time. Even if Wren is in Reno, that doesn't mean Don has taken Honor there, too."

Wilder doesn't appear happy with the answer. "No, but if we find Wren, he might know where Don would have taken her."

Rafferty blows the air out of his lungs. "You say that as though finding Wren is an easy thing to do. Haven't we been trying for years? He's as slippery as an eel, and the moment he gets wind that someone is onto him, he'll vanish again. If we show up in Reno and start asking questions, I guarantee it'll get back to him, and then he'll be gone and so will our chance of finding Don and Honor. Let Carter do his job."

Wilder folds his massive arms. "What are we supposed to do, then? Sit around here, twiddling our thumbs?"

"We still have other leads we can follow. We can find out what Don's driving, and if the boat has been registered at any marinas. There's a chance he even took Honor back to his home address, though I doubt he'd want to shit on his own doorstep."

Wilder growls. "I want to get out there."

"I know you do, but that's not going to help Honor any."

It's time for Asher and me to leave, so we say goodbye to the others and promise to stay in touch. We're going to need to get the seaplane over to the mainland and then take one of the vehicles we have parked over there. It's a good six to seven hours' drive, depending on traffic.

"Oh, and Asher?" Rafferty adds.

Asher pauses and turns to him.

Rafferty continues. "Don't go getting yourself arrested."

Asher grins. "I'm smarter than that."

Chapter Seven
Honor

I DON'T WANT TO TAKE a shower.

I thought I could do this, so full of inner bravado while outside, but now, in the house, just me and Don…it's a lot more intimidating than I had imagined.

I run the water and stand in the middle of the bathroom, still fully clothed. I'm hugely conscious of Don on the other side of the door. He's said he'll give me some privacy, but I'm not naïve enough to believe that's the truth. Not after I teased him, for sure. God, what was I thinking? My bravery seems to have vanished.

My heart flutters, and my pulse seems to be bouncing around inside my veins. I'm lightheaded from lack of sleep and the adrenaline flooding my system. It all makes it hard to think straight. To focus.

I need to stay alive long enough for them to find me, but perhaps my earlier idea about seducing Don was stupid, as well as naïve as to how easy I would find it. If I give him what he wants, he won't have anything to keep me around for. Will he?

Despite the numerous locks on the front door—ones Don must have installed himself, as I can't imagine any normal rental needing to provide that kind of security—there is a distinct lack of them on the bathroom door. A groove in the wood above the door handle indicates a spot where a simple sliding bolt must have been jimmied off. There isn't even a chair in the room that I can use to wedge under the handle, but again, I expect that's deliberate.

A frosted glass window is to my left, and I go to it, hoping to find a way out. If I have to jump from a second story window in order to escape, then that's exactly what I'll do. Maybe I'll break my legs and be in an even worse position than I am now, but at least I'll have tried to run. I could wrap a towel around me and try to break the glass, as I've seen that in TV shows, but the glass is double thickness and I doubt I could do it without breaking something. There's also the question of the noise repeated attempts would make. Noise which would alert Don to what I am trying to do.

The window isn't going to provide my escape, however. It only opens at the top and is too narrow for me to fit through. I could try to break the rest of the window, but there's nothing in the room for me to use. Other than the toiletries bottles and the towels and bathmat, everything else is attached to the floor. I'm in no way strong enough to wrench up a toilet or sink and use it to smash the glass.

The room is filling with steam.

I'm still shaking, cold to the bone with both fear and the long trip exposed in the boat. The thought of a hot shower is inviting, and Don is going to be able to tell if I don't take one. Then he'll question why I've lied to him. He has every reason to be suspicious of me. Haven't I spent the last few months doing everything I can to escape him?

No normal person would think for a single second that I'd be interested in him that way, but Don isn't a normal person. He's got an ego the size of the Arctic, and deep down, he believes everyone should love him, including me.

But he also knows that *I* know what he's capable of.

Murder.

Feeling I have little choice, I quickly strip off my clothes and hang them on the ladder-style radiator to dry out. I yank my hair into a high knot—not wanting it to get wet again—and step under the hot spray.

The jets of hot water pummel my tense muscles, and I exhale the air from my lungs and relax, just a fraction, for the first time in hours. I close my eyes and picture myself back at the resort, in my own bathroom. The memory has my eyes pricking with tears.

I'm still haunted by the death of Edwardo and the knowledge that I'm with a man who thinks nothing of shooting someone. I've always known Don is dangerous—he killed my mother—but having it happen right in front of me like that has rocked me to my core. I can't help blaming myself, too. If I hadn't persuaded him to help me, Edwardo would still be alive. I want to convince myself that Edwardo must have been as bad as Don if he was working with him, but Don is a master manipulator, and he doesn't only hold that influence over the women in his life.

Over the water hitting the stall, I hear the crack of the door opening, and the change in the air as steam is released. I don't want to look, because it will only confirm what I already know—that Don has entered the bathroom.

I should have known he wouldn't keep his promise.

I lean out of the shower to grab a towel from the heated rail to cover myself, but he's too quick for me, and he whips it out of my reach.

"Now, now, Honor," he says. "You know I like to watch. I think maybe you like it too, if your earlier words were anything to go by."

I'm on a tightrope right now. Give this man enough to keep him invested, but not too much. I use my hands to cover my body as best I can—one hand and forearm across my breasts, flattening them, the other hiding my pussy. My back curves like a bow as I hunch to try to protect my naked form from his gaze. It's a natural instinct, but also something I think he will like because he's sick.

"Soap yourself down," he instructs.

His lips part, and his tongue flicks out to swipe across his lower lip. His eyes darken with raw lust, and a whimper escapes my lips, and not one I have to force; it's entirely natural. I'm such a fool. Did I really think myself capable of seducing this man?

"Do it."

"No." My voice is barely a squeak.

"Do it, or I'll join you in there and do it myself."

I don't doubt for a second that he will keep his word. I picture him stripping off and joining me in here, of him shoving me up against the tiled wall, and taking me from behind. I'll do whatever it takes to stop that from happening.

With a shaking hand, I lift a bottle of lemon-scented shower gel from the toiletries holder attached to the wall in the corner of the shower. It takes me a moment to flick open the plastic cap. The bottle is new. I tip it upside down and pour some of the fragrant, citrus soap into the palm of my other hand.

"Stand up straight," Don commands. "Soap those titties up nice and good."

I don't look at him as I do it, running my soapy palm over my chest.

"Cup them, squeeze them," he says. "Make it hot."

I feel sick, but I do as he says. I need to go somewhere else in my mind, so I do. I'm no longer in this tawdry bathroom but on the island, with my men. My nipples grow hard beneath my caresses, and my core pulses in response, my stomach muscles tightening.

"Now call me that name again. The one you used before you came into the bathroom."

"Daddy," I whisper.

He's rubbing himself over his jeans. "That's right. My good girl."

The bulge in his pants is clear. Is this it? Is he going to take his cock out and fuck me now? I tell myself I'll take my mind somewhere else if he does. I'll pretend it's not happening to me. I won't let myself feel a thing.

But Don isn't done with the show.

"Now turn around and bend over and wash your ass and pussy. Spread those legs."

At least facing away from him means I won't have to look at him, and I can carry on with my fantasy of it being the men watching me, not him. I pick up the shower gel and squeeze more into my palm, careful not to let the water wash it away, and set the bottle down again.

A tear trickles down my cheek. I use one hand to brace myself against the shower wall, my fingers splayed against the cream tile, and the other soaps my ass cheeks. From behind, I run my fingers run between my legs, over my folds. I experience a tightening of arousal, of heat building. I don't want to climax, even if it's only at my own hand, but this way it keeps him satisfied with a show, and my time on the island has left my body primed for pleasure. The crest that was once so hard to ride is now quite literally at my fingertips. All I have to do is think of them, and I can find that elusive pleasure.

Over the steady thrum of water, Don's breathing grows harsher. I can hear his movements, the jangle of a belt buckle being knocked repetitively by a hand, the rustle of clothing, and a grunt of pleasure. I know he's masturbating, but I don't look. I prefer not to have my suspicions confirmed.

Instead, I imagine it's the others watching me with their cocks out —Asher, Brody, Wilder and Rafferty. I'd be more than happy for any of them to get off on seeing me do this. I'm just thankful Don hasn't touched me yet, but I'm sure he's building himself up to it. Maybe he just wants to eke out my torment, and his pleasure.

The soap has all washed away now, but he doesn't tell me to stop touching myself. I stick out my ass and rub my pussy from behind, dipping my fingers into my wet heat. My clit tingles and pulses, needing to be touched, but I don't want to give Don any ideas.

A gasp and a grunt come from behind me, but I do my best to ignore it and focus inward. My belly tightens to a knot, my pussy pulsing. My nipples are hard bullets, and I arch my back so they touch the cold tile in a sensation close to pain. I thrust my fingers inside myself, imaging it's Rafferty's touch I feel, or perhaps Wilder's. Someone I feel safe with.

It's a strange orgasm that my body eventually gives in to. It's nothing like the mind shattering ones I've experienced with the men. It's more of a whimper than a scream, and my body rolls with it, my eyes squeezed shut, my core clenching around nothing. It leaves me feeling dirty and a little nauseated, and I sink against the cold tile wall, grateful for the support.

"Turn off the water," Don says.

I still don't want to look. I think he's come, but there's a good chance I'm going to turn around and find him half undressed with his cock in his hand. This might have just been the warmup. But I switch off the shower. My legs are weak beneath me, my skin pink. Bizarrely, as I turn to face him, I cover myself up again with my hands. I don't know why I bother, considering he's been staring at my most intimate parts for the last five minutes, but I can't help myself.

When I eventually force my eyes to lift to Don, he's standing there, fully dressed, as though nothing has happened. He holds a large gray towel, spread out, between both hands, and it's clear he expects me to step into it.

Though I don't want to accept anything he offers me, I'd rather be wrapped in a towel than standing here, naked and exposed. I step out of the shower, and he folds me within the fluffy, warm material and then kisses me chastely on the top of the head. The heat of his breath warms my scalp as he lingers.

"Good girl."

I try not to shudder at his touch.

"This way."

I clutch my towel tight to the spot between my breasts. He keeps his arm around my shoulders as he guides me out of the bathroom, down the hall, to a bedroom. My gaze takes in the sparseness of the room—just a bare mattress in the middle of the floor. I open my mouth, though I'm not totally sure what I want to say, but he plants his palm in the middle of my back, where my skin is still damp from the shower, and shoves me inside.

I almost stumble but manage to hang on to the towel. I spin to face him, but the door slams shut behind me, and a click signals a lock being driven into place.

I could go to the door and bang on it with my fists and scream to be let out, but what would be the point? At least in here, I'm separated from Don by a locked door and these walls. I look around, hoping for some clothes to materialize, but there's nothing—not even a closet to look inside. I guess I'm lucky he let me keep the towel. As there's nothing on the bed—not even a bottom sheet. It will serve as my blanket as well as my clothes.

Outside the window, the sky is starting to lighten, the rising sun pushing back the night. The stars vanish, the dark indigo fading to a kind of hazy gray. We're on the second story, and I know without checking that the windows will all be locked. Just like with the bathroom, there's nothing in the room I can use to break the glass. I still go to it, though, hoping the view outside might give me some idea about where I am. But all I can see, spreading all directions, are rows and rows of vineyards, vanishing off into the hills.

I could be anywhere.

Exhausted, I go to the mattress on the floor and curl up on my side, drawing my knees to my chest, as though I'm a small child. Shame at what just happened washes over me. Have I betrayed the others by giving in to Don? Should I have fought? There wouldn't have been any point. If I hadn't gone along with what he wanted, he only would have made things harder on me. But that doesn't wash away the guilt I'm now drowning under.

My shoulders shake as I give in to tears.

Chapter Eight
Asher

I DRIVE FAST, NOT CARING about the speed limit. I almost want to get pulled over by the cops. Right now, every cop represents Detective Don Bowen, and the urge to take my anger out on one of them boils beneath the surface.

The sun is rising now, and there's no sign of the rainstorm that hit the island last night. That we're starting a new day without Honor in our lives is something I don't want to think about. At least the early hour means the roads are quiet. There isn't too much traffic to contend with, though that's going to change the moment we get near the city.

Brody sits in the passenger seat, his body twisted to watch the scenery go by. We're both silent, lost in our own worlds of fear for what might be happening to Honor.

It's a special kind of torture, and, as much as I don't want to think, I can't help it. Fury and a crazy kind of jealousy churn within me like a silent storm.

With each hour that passes, my frustration mounts. I don't even want to stop for bathroom breaks, or to get gas, but they are necessary evils on a drive of this length. We make a quick stop and grab coffee and a couple of breakfast sandwiches and then get on the road again.

"Anything?" I ask Brody as I catch him from the corner of my eye checking his cell phone.

He shakes his head. "Not yet."

"Fuck."

We left the other two chasing things from their end, contacting local marinas and car rentals, trying to find out if anyone matching Don's description was spotted or if they had the name of the boat logged anywhere.

"What about the PI?" I ask.

Brody blows out a breath. "It's only been a few hours, man. Give him the chance to do his job."

I want to snap back, but I clench my jaw and grind my teeth instead. A part of me is still resentful of Brody for putting us all in this situation in the first place, but then I remind myself that if Don knew Honor's location, it only would have been a matter of time before he took her. Besides, him finding out where she was is on me.

I grip the steering wheel, tight enough that my knuckles become shiny, white balls. One thing tortures me even more than the thought of Honor with her stepfather, and that's Honor with Pastor Wren. I tell myself that Wren would have no interest in her—after all, she's far too old for his tastes, and she's female—but the damage he caused me in childhood is still so fresh in my mind, it's as though just the thought of him being with Honor is enough to make me endure it afresh.

The higher the sun rises, the more color seeps back into the world around us. The number of other vehicles we've passed has been sporadic, but now they're increasing. I picture us stuck in traffic in downtown LA and want to roar with the frustration of it. But what choice do we have?

After another couple of hours, we make another bathroom stop at a gas station and I fill up the car. We still haven't heard anything from either the PI, or Rafferty and Wilder.

It feels like a dangerously large amount of time has passed by the time we hit the outskirts of Los Angeles and merge with the city traffic. A part of me wants to dump the car and walk the rest, but it's still too far. Instead, I endure it, and keep pushing forward, driving aggressively to push into any gap I can find. I ignore the blasts of horns that follow me, people signaling their annoyance—they mean nothing to me.

Rush hour is over by the time we reach the Los Angeles Police Department. Someone must be smiling down on us, as I find a parking spot right away.

We already know we're not going to find Don at his precinct—a phone call the other day confirmed that he's on vacation—but I assume he has a partner who wouldn't be allowed to take time off as well. I have no idea if anyone will talk to me, but I do have a duffle bag filled with cash in the trunk, and I'll use it to get information if I have to.

"Wait here," I tell Brody.

I don't need to explain why. The two of us going in together will draw attention. One of my strengths is that I can slide under the radar.

I climb out of the car and slam the door shut behind me. The street is busy, and after the relative isolation of the island, it feels overwhelming. Some people are suited and walk briskly, while others are dressed in casual clothes and linger to take selfies. The imposing building opposite rises into a clear blue sky, and palm trees surrounding it flutter in the breeze. The sight of the black and white police cars put me on edge, and I have to remind myself that I'm not the criminal here.

I straighten my shirt and trot up the steps to the tall glass and stone building. Inside, the much cooler air is a blessed relief from the Los Angeles sun, and I head straight to the reception desk where a female desk sergeant is manning it.

She gives me a polite smile. "Can I help you?"

"I need to speak to someone about Don Bowen."

"Detective Bowen?" she confirms.

"That's right."

"Can I ask what this is concerning?"

"It's concerning the location of his stepdaughter. I'm afraid I can't say more than that, unless it's to someone close to him. I believe his partner may be in today."

"Detective Murphy," she says. "Let me just check. Who can I say is here?"

I give a fake surname. "Ash Shanley."

"One minute, please."

I step back to allow her to place the call. She says a few words, her gaze flicking over to me, and then just as quickly back down to desk. Does she think I'm a criminal? I'd have to have some big balls to walk right into a police station if I was.

She ends the call and addresses me. "If you'd like to take a seat, he'll be out shortly."

I cross the polished floor to a bank of chairs and sit with my elbows on my knees, my spine at a forty-five-degree angle. I tap my fingers together and do my best to keep my ass wedged to the plastic chair so I don't end up pacing. People will remember an agitated man stomping around, and I want to go as unnoticed as possible.

A man in a suit approaches, drawing my attention.

"Ash Shanley?" he asks.

I rise to my feet. "That's right."

Don Bowen's partner is a black man with a shaved head and broad shoulders. I put him to be in his forties, but he could be ten years north or south from there.

"I'm Detective Murphy," he says. "What can I do for you?"

I'm aware of how this big LAPD detective sees me. My compact frame. The glasses. The serious expression. He doesn't take me to be anything of a threat.

"Don Bowen is your partner, right?" I ask.

He jerks his chin in a nod. "That's right."

"I need to speak to you about him. About what he's been up to."

He assesses me anew. "In which case, I suggest we go through to an interview room."

I hold his gaze. "Are you sure you want to do that?" If this man is aware of what sort of person his partner is, he's not going to want any of this conversation recorded. "I thought it might be better if we talk in the bar across the road."

He purses his lips, but still, I don't look away.

"Trust me when I say you're going to want to talk to me."

"Okay, Mr. Shanley. I'll meet you over there in ten."

I turn and walk from the station and go back to Brody in the car. "He's agreed to meet us."

Brody climbs out. "Good. Let's hope our instincts are right with this one."

"I think they are."

I go to the trunk and take out the duffle bag containing a large sum of cash I'd taken from the safe back at the resort before we left. I pause, unzip the bag and take out a couple of bundles of bills, and then lift the base of the trunk and slide the money in with the spare tire. We might need it sometime.

I slam the trunk shut and lift the bag, which is still heavy with cash, and swing it onto my shoulder. "Let's go."

We go to the bar I'd indicated to Detective Murphy and find a table in the corner. It's still early and the place is empty. Music plays in the background, and the lighting is low, despite the bright day outside. The table between us is sticky with spilled beer and needs wiping.

We have time to order coffee, and then Detective Murphy enters. He glances around and spots us. His eyes narrow at the sight of Brody—he'd obviously thought it was just going to be the two of us—but he comes over anyway.

"Who's this?" he asks.

Brody jerks his head. "I'm Brody. That's all you need to know."

Murphy arches an eyebrow. "I'll be the judge of that."

He takes a seat opposite, and the bartender arrives with the coffees. I assume it isn't normally table service in here, but the place is practically empty. Only an old man sits on a stool at the bar, and he isn't paying any attention to us.

The detective sits back and folds his arms across his thick chest. "What's this all about?"

I jump straight in. "We have reason to believe Detective Bowen is corrupt. He's been taking money in exchange for letting drug dealers off the hook."

His expression remains unreadable. "Is this something you have proof of?"

"Yes. I have some of the money he took." Under the table, I nudge the bag with my foot.

Dangling this kind of money in front of someone is going to be a surefire way of finding out if they're susceptible to taking it in return for answering some questions. Of course, I also have to be careful. I don't want to end up being arrested for trying to bribe a police officer, but I tend to think of myself as a fairly good judge of character, and my gut is telling me that Detective Murphy is as bent as his partner.

"How did you get that?" Murphy asks.

"We know his stepdaughter. She ran away from him and took this money with her. She told us Don got it from receiving bribes from people, which was why she didn't feel bad taking it." This is all a lie, but he isn't to know that.

"Why isn't his stepdaughter telling us this herself?"

There was no point in lying about this part. "Because she's with Don—against her will."

"And she just happened to leave this amount of money with you? Why?"

"Don didn't give her much choice."

"If you're worried for the safety of this young woman, you need to leave it in our hands."

Brody cocks an eyebrow. "Why? Because you've done such a good job of keeping her safe so far? You know she reported that Don killed her mother."

Murphy is naturally protective of his partner. "The girl was hysterical. There was no such evidence of that happening. The poor woman fell down the stairs."

Brody snorts. "If you say so."

I take over. "Here's the thing. We don't care about Don being corrupt. We literally couldn't give a shit. All we want is to make sure his stepdaughter is okay. We can leave this bag of cash on the floor, right here beside the chair, and walk out. No one needs to know we ever brought it in. But in return, we need some info on Don."

The other man doesn't balk. He doesn't appear horrified at the suggestion. He also doesn't attempt to arrest us for bribery. "What kind of info?"

"We want you to request his bank and credit card records. We need to find out where he is, and if he's used his card recently. If he's rented a car, we need to know the make and model and the license plate number."

Murphy purses his lips again. "When do you need this by?"

"ASAP." I think of something and shrug. "Unless you know where Don is, of course, and where he might have taken his stepdaughter, and you can tell us yourself."

"He's on vacation as far as I know. Mexico."

I wince. "I already know that's not true."

"What can I say? It's what he told me and the rest of the department."

"In which case, we're definitely going to need those bank records, 'cause that's bullshit."

Murphy rubs two fingers across his lips and glances down at the bag. "Can I see how much is in there?"

I lean down and unzip it. "Be my guest."

He checks the contents and then straightens. "Okay. Give me your number, and I'll contact you as soon as I have the information."

I shake my head. "No numbers." Cell phones can be traced, and I have no intention of leaving a trail. "Get the information. We'll be waiting here, with the money."

"It may take a while."

"In which case, sitting here might get expensive. I imagine ten grand an hour expensive."

Brody steps in, his tone filled with tension. "So I suggest you work quickly. You'll get the money once it's done."

He pauses for a moment, looking as though he's considering arguing with us, but then he nods and gets to his feet. No one says another word as the detective turns from us and leaves the dark, dingy bar.

Now, we wait.

Chapter Nine
Honor

I'M LYING ON THE HUGE bed in my room at the resort. I'm on my back, my arms and legs spread in the shape of a star. Something fastens each of my ankles and wrists to the corners of the bed so I'm unable to move. I'm acutely aware of the fact I'm completely naked. I'm already aroused, my body needy and aching. My nipples are hard, tight buds, and I squirm against the mattress, trying to get some relief. But the way my limbs are spread means I can't press my thighs together.

I let out a whimper.

For reasons I don't understand, I haven't tried to move my head to discover if there's anyone else in the room with me. Instead, I stare up at the ceiling, focusing on a tiny spot of damp. Small patches of gray and black mold are forming, the spores spreading in almost snowflake-like patterns.

The first flicker of unease trembles within me. Since when does any part of the resort have mold? The place is meticulously maintained.

A voice startles me from my thoughts.

"Honor?"

My heart leaps. "Rafferty?"

Finally, I look away from the ceiling, down the length of my body, between the twin mounds of breasts and through my spread legs.

He's standing there with his suit jacket and tie removed, his shirt sleeves rolled up, his top button open. He's staring down at me with lust in his eyes, and I almost want to cry at the beauty of him. God, he's so perfect.

"Rafferty, why am I tied up?"

My voice sounds strange, distant, as though I'm listening to a recording of myself.

"You know why."

I shake my head. "No, I don't."

"It's so you can't get away when I lick your pussy."

My breath catches, and a wave of desire pulses through me. "Oh."

I'm not going to argue with him about that.

He moves slowly, keeping eye contact with me the whole time. I'm locked into his gaze, even as the bed dips with his weight, and he lowers his face between my thighs. I feel the heat of his breath first, and that alone has me wanting to cry out, to lift my hips and press myself to him. Wetness trickles out of me, and he's there to catch it on his tongue.

I twist my face to the side, unable to watch any longer—the sensations are so intense—and standing to my right is Brody.

His expression is troubled. "I'm sorry," he says. "I shouldn't have frightened you like that. This is all my fault."

I don't understand what he means. What's his fault? The way Rafferty's tongue is curling around my clit makes it hard for me to keep my thoughts straight.

BROKEN LIMITS

That same sense of unease as when I'd seen the mold goes though me. Have I forgotten something?

I try to reach out to Brody, wanting to take his hand and pull him down onto the bed beside me, but I've forgotten that I'm tied down.

Then Rafferty moves his attention from my pussy to my ass, and I yelp in surprise. His tongue probes me, pushing past the tight ring and into my channel. I buck my hip and squeal.

"I want to get in there," a voice says, but it's not Rafferty speaking.

I blink and try to sit. Rafferty has gone, and in his place is Wilder.

"Where—where did Rafferty go?"

How did I not noticed them switching?

Wilder frowns. "What are you talking about? It was always me."

My mind blurs with confusion. My body aches with need. I'm desperate to reach a climax, but there's a strange sensation taking over me, like a memory that I can't quite place. I want to come, but the sensation brings a different feeling with it, one of disgust at myself. Is it because he's playing with my ass? That's never bothered me in such a way before.

Wilder is unaware of my inner turmoil. He'd paused licking me to talk, but now he goes back down. My breath comes short and ragged, and I chase my orgasm, every muscle in my body winding tighter like a spring.

Then he stops, and I want to cry, "No!"

Wilder shifts his position, so he's on his knees, his huge cock in his hand. The metal piercings look even scarier than before. "I'm going to fuck you in the ass, Honor. I'm going to take you hard and fast."

"No," I say again, but this time for a different reason. "You'll hurt me."

"A little pain is good, right?"

Maybe a little pain, but Wilder's cock in my ass could do some damage.

"No, please. You can't."

But he's shifting into position, and with my ankles and wrists bound, there's nothing I can do about it.

"Help!" I cry. "Someone help me."

A hand touches my face from my left, and I whip my head around. Asher is here now.

"Asher, please, stop him. He's going to hurt me."

Asher gives a faint laugh. "Silly girl. Wilder would never hurt you."

But the head of Wilder's cock presses at my hole. The metal of his piercing is cold against my heated flesh. I want him to stop, but that gnawing, aching, insistent need to come won't leave me alone.

Then he's stretching me, wider than I'd ever thought was possible. I scream, but it's more from fear than pain. And with my scream, so the mold on the ceiling suddenly bursts to life, spreading like wildfire across the ceiling. It reaches the point where the wall meets the ceiling, and the luxurious wallpaper curls at the edges and then strips down as though some invisible person is tearing at it. The room seems to dissolve around me. The big, soft bed vanishes, replaced by uneven, cold concrete. The ceiling is concrete too now, and I find myself in the dark.

I suddenly realize where I am.

I'm back in the bunker.

I can no longer feel Wilder pressing his way into me. All I can hear is my own breath, loud in my ears.

"Wilder?" I cry. "Asher? Brody? Rafferty?"

Someone else's voice greets me. "They're not here."

My blood freezes, and I go completely still.

It's Don.

He moves closer—I can sense the heat of his body and his overwhelming presence.

"There's something you want, isn't there?" he asks. "Something you're craving?"

I don't react.

Cold fingers push inside me. Two are in my pussy, and his little finger slides inside my ass. I buck and whimper. I don't want him touching me, but it feels so good and I need to come.

"That's right, little girl," he says. "Come for Daddy. Let me feel that sweet pussy gush all over my fingers. Daddy's little princess."

I'm repulsed and turned on in equal measures. I know I should push him away, but I can't. I'm purely focused on reaching my climax, and I barrel toward it. Just as I'm on the brink, he leans closer and speaks against my ear.

"Your cunt is even sweeter than your mother's."

I BURST UPRIGHT, GASPING for breath, my skin soaked in sweat.

The bare mattress is beneath me, and I'm still naked, only the towel covering my body. Crazily, the promise of an orgasm in my dream continues to linger, and I press my thighs together and let out a sob.

It's fully light outside now. A new day.

Will it be my last?

God, that dream somehow managed to be both sexy and horrific, all at the same time. That it might also be a very real representation of what my near future holds also makes me want to cry.

I have to do something. I can't just sit here and wait until Don decides he wants to fuck me for real. I need to try to escape.

But I don't even have any clothes. The door is locked, as is the window, and I don't have anything I can use to break the glass. My only hope for escape is out the front door, ideally with the car keys, so I can drive the hell away from here. But I'll have to get through Don first, and he's armed and has already proven he's more than happy to commit murder, if he has to.

What about me, I wonder. Could I kill, if it came down to it? Could I take that gun from Don's hand and turn it around on him and pull the trigger? I reach deep inside me for the anger I've been harboring for so long and test its strength. If I had to take an innocent person's life, I don't think I could live with myself, but Don is far from innocent.

Maybe killing him will change me forever. Maybe that won't be such a bad thing.

Footsteps approach on the other side of the door, shortly followed by the click of locks being drawn back.

I gather the towel around my body and push back with my heels until my back hits the farthest corner of the room. The wall is cold against my skin, but I barely notice. All my attention is on the door.

The handle turns, and it opens. Don steps into the room. He's carrying a couple of brown paper bags with him. The scent of coffee fills the room, and I feel myself awaken with it.

"Sleep well?" he asks.

I don't bother to reply, and only scowl in return and hold the towel closer. My gaze darts beyond him, to where he's left the door open. Can I get past him and make a run for it? I want to try, but there's only a matter of an arm's length between him and the doorway, and if I run, he'll grab me easily.

I remember my promise to myself yesterday about making him believe I'm on his side, of seducing him and lulling him into a false sense of security, but now I'm in this position, I'm finding it a lot harder than I'd imagined.

Still, I force myself play along. "Better than I'd expected."

He smiles. "Did you dream about me, Honor?"

My cheeks instantly flame with heat. There's no possible way he can know about my dreams, but it's as though he's reaching inside my head and plucked them from my brain.

I need to change the subject, and I jerk my chin at the bags. "Did you bring me something? I smell coffee."

He glances down at the bags, as though he'd forgotten he was holding them. "Oh, yes. Coffee and a pastry. I remembered what you like—those little flaky almond croissants."

He sets one of the bags down in front of me, then takes a step back. It makes me feel like I'm an animal in a zoo and he's the keeper. The pastry and coffee are an offering to stop me from attacking.

I note the logo on the front of the paper bag and the coffee cup. The coffee is still warm, and the pastry seems fresh. When I'd looked out of the window, and during the drive here, I'd believed we were in the middle of nowhere, but now I'm thinking differently. If Don left the house this morning to drive to get coffee and pastries while I was sleeping, then there must be a coffeeshop or a bakery somewhere nearby. If there's a coffeeshop, then it also means there must be a population it serves.

Hot and Steamy Coffee.

I imprint the name of the place on my brain.

"There's a second bag," Don says, holding it out to me. "Something for you to wear."

I'm happy to have the chance to get dressed, but this bag clearly doesn't hold the items I'd arrived here in. It's far too small and doesn't look as though it weighs much at all.

Tentatively, I put out a hand, and he gives the bag to me. I withdraw into my corner, my legs tucked beneath me, my other hand still holding the towel. I reach into the bag and pluck out the item.

My stomach sinks.

It's a baby doll negligée in pink with a satin bow at the point between the lacy cups. I realize that a simple tug on that bow will allow the whole thing to fall open. It's floating and swirly, but also almost see-through. It's a weird combination of being extremely sexy while also being somehow childlike.

I hate it instantly.

"Put it on," Don says. "The others will be here soon."

My blood runs cold. "Others. What others?"

He doesn't give me a straight answer. "I think you're going to be a little old for their taste, but we can always lie and say you're younger. Looking as you do right now, with no makeup and naked as the day you were born, I'd say you could pass for seventeen."

I almost don't want to know. "Seventeen? Why do I need to be seventeen?"

"Let's just say this group of men prefer their pussy to be untouched, innocent. Young."

A wave of nausea washes over me. Is Don saying what I think he's saying? Is he about to hand me over to a bunch of fucking pervs? I'd thought my situation was bad enough, but it's just gotten a thousand times worse. Maybe I would have been able to handle Don fucking me—I'd have been traumatized, but I'd figure out a way to live with it—but being handed around to men like that? Would they all want a turn? Was that to be my fate?

Even though I'm sitting, I need to put a hand to the wall to steady myself. The room spins around me. This is sick. This whole fucking thing is sick.

I have badly misjudged what is going on here. The man isn't deeply in love with me, not if he's willing to pass me around like a toy.

I send a silent prayer out to Rafferty and the others. *Please find me. Please, please, please. Find me before it's too late.*

This explains the baby doll negligée. He's dressing me up for these fuckers.

There was me thinking Don would be possessive of me, that he'd want me for himself, when the whole time he'd been planning on sharing me around. This is so different from being back at the resort, I can't even get my head around it. Yes, I was shared between Rafferty, Brody, Asher, and Wilder—and maybe it wasn't always willingly at first, other than for the money —but they always made sure I was satisfied sexually, and they always turned me on. I dread to think what kind of men I'm about to be handed to.

I need to be brave. Cowering and simpering in a corner isn't going to get me anywhere.

I don't know if these men will like it better if I'm meek and compliant, or if they'll get turned if I try to fight, but I decide I won't let them take me easily. If I can draw some blood first, then I will.

Unsteadily, I get to my feet. I set my jaw and put my shoulders back and take a step closer to Don. I hold his eye, hoping he can see the fire burning inside me.

"I'll tell them the truth. I'll tell them how old I am, and I'll make sure they know I'm far from being untouched."

His eyes harden. "You shut your mouth, princess."

"Why? Because you don't want to hear the truth? I've been more than touched. I've had four men fuck me all at the same time. I've sucked their cocks and they've fucked my mouth and come down my throat. I've had two of them inside me at the same time, one in my ass and one in my pussy, and they made me come harder than I knew was even possible." I spit the words at him. "And do you know what? I loved every second of it."

The crack across my cheekbone sends my head rocking backward, and I find myself back on the floor. I don't even feel any pain for a moment. I'm too busy seeing stars and trying to figure out what's just happened.

Don is standing over me, his finger jabbed in my direction. "Don't ever let me hear you speak like that again, or you'll get a lot worse than a slap on the face. You got it?"

So, he slapped me. That makes sense. The restraint he'd had when he slapped me shortly after our arrival has vanished. He didn't hold back this time.

I give my head a slight shake—not to indicate no, but to try to dislodge the ringing that's suddenly started in my ear on the side where he hit me. Heat blooms in the shapes of his fingers, and I wonder if he'll have left a bruise. Maybe not. He's clever. He knows just how to hit to prevent visible bruising—or at least he did with my mother. He never wanted anyone asking any difficult questions. Of course, Don doesn't care if he leaves a mark on my face now. No one is going to see it, at least, no one who'll care.

I stay where I am, waiting for the darkness around the edges of my vision to fade. It occurs to me that I may have inadvertently found Don's weak spot. He still wants to think of me as the young girl I once was—untouched, pure. He can't stand the thought that I've been defiled by anyone other than him. Or perhaps it's not for himself. Is it these 'others' he's mentioned a couple of times now? Was there some kind of agreement that he'd deliver me to them still a virgin?

The possibility is weighty on my mind. It might also explain why he didn't just take me in the shower—why he didn't even touch me. Perhaps he worried that if he got started, he wouldn't be able to stop himself from taking me.

Is there someone he's trying to impress? Someone he wants to make an impact on? Someone who might be coming here?

I don't push Don any further. I'm worried I'll end up with a boot in the stomach, or worse. Instead, I stay huddled on the floor and pray that he'll leave.

"Get dressed," he says from above me. "Then drink your coffee and eat your food, and, if you're lucky, I'll let you use the bathroom. But if you misbehave like that again, I'll have you pissing in the corner. Do you understand me?"

I don't look up, but I nod. My heart is racing like a tribal beat, my ears are still ringing, and all I want is for him to leave.

A few moments pass, and then I hear the click of the locks sliding into place again.

I sink back against the wall and allow myself to breathe.

Chapter Ten
Rafferty

MY PHONE RINGS, AND I snatch it up.

"Rafferty, it's Carter," the person on the end of the line says.

"What have you found?" I ask.

"I'm still working on it, but the person I suspected of being Wren left already."

"Fuck!" I curse. "Does anyone know where he's gone? Has he left permanently, or is he coming back?"

"Unsure about that, currently."

Frustration and anger boil inside me. "Unsure? I don't pay you to be unsure. I pay you to find out facts."

Every minute that goes by is another minute Honor is taken farther from us, and it'll be harder to find her. I can't even allow myself to think about what her stepfather might be doing to her. If I allow my thoughts to linger on it, the rage grows within me, and I think I could lose my mind.

"Like I said, I'm still working on it. I did manage to get a picture, however. I'm sending it to your phone right now."

My phone buzzes, and I take it away from my ear to check the message I've just been sent. I open it, and the sight is like a punch to my solar plexus.

It's him. Wren. He's older now—in his sixties instead of his thirties, as he had been when I'd known him—but his face is unmistakable. It's all in the eyes and the curl of those cruel lips.

I hate that my hand is shaking when I lift the phone back to my ear. "That's him."

"You sure?" Carter asks.

"One hundred percent. Where did you get the photo?"

"I asked one of the volunteers at the church. Wren is normally careful about having his photograph taken. He doesn't want people posting his image online—or anywhere else, for that matter. I said I was a reporter and writing an article on inspiring preachers, but that I'd been unable to track down any photographs, and she admitted she'd snapped a quick pic at a church gathering a few weeks ago. It had taken a little greasing of the palm to get her to send it to me, but she did eventually."

No one is immune to the power of green, it seems. Even those who consider themselves to be devout still fold when there is enough money involved.

"Well done," I say, but there is a tremor in my voice, and I clear my throat. "At least now we have confirmation. Keep asking around. Find out what car he's driving or if he was traveling with anyone else."

"Will do. If I can find out the car registration, I might be able to get the local police to do a lookout on the plate. They have automatic license plate recognition technology on traffic cameras now, so we might get lucky and pick it up."

"Good. Grease their palms with however much money it takes. No sum is too large. Got it?"

"Got it."

I end the call and toss the phone back down on the desk. I exhale a long breath and rub both hands across my face. I can't believe we've lost Wren right after we found him again, though I'm hoping its only temporary.

We have no way of knowing if Wren has gone to join Honor and Detective Don somewhere, but there's a possibility. I'm not going to ignore any leads at this point. If he doesn't have anything to do with Don or Honor, then as soon as we get Honor back, I'm going to make it a priority that we find Wren and finish that asshole once and for all.

Wilder enters the room, his head down. He sees me sitting there and comes to a halt.

"What's happened?"

"Wren left Reno. We don't know where he's gone or if it's for good."

Wilder grabs a chair and drags it over to sit opposite me. "It was definitely him, then?"

I pick my phone back up and push it at him, the photograph open on screen. I watch Wilder—all six feet four of him, with his piercings and tats and long hair—somehow shrink. It's like seeing that picture reduces us to our childlike state, the boys we'd once been. I understand exactly how he's feeling, the churning in his stomach, the rapid rate of his pulse. I understand how, even so many years later, he's filled with shame and sickened at the things Wren made us so.

Fury at how the image of this man has reduced my strong, powerful friend fills me afresh. That Wren might also somehow be connected to Honor's kidnapping also helps stoke the fire.

Wilder takes the phone from me, and I notice his hand tremble.

"Fuck. He doesn't look any different."

"Just a little older," I comment.

Wilder stares at the phone a few seconds longer and then hands it back. "Do you think he'd recognize any of us now, if he saw us?"

"Honestly, I don't know. I mean, how many of us have there been? Plus, we've all changed so much."

Wilder presses his lips into a thin line. "I don't think his ego would allow him to recognize us. He'd never believe we'd come back for revenge. He'd never think we were capable of it."

"You're probably right, but we'll prove him wrong."

"You heard anything from Asher and Brody yet?" Wilder asks.

"They're waiting for some information. They said they'll be in touch when they have it."

Wilder pushes back his chair and gets to his feet. "And what are we going to do in the meantime? I can't keep sitting around like this."

He's right. "I think we need to get ready to make a move, and to be able to move fast."

Wilder narrows his eyes at me. "What are you getting at?"

"Let's make sure the birds are ready to take to the sky."

Chapter Eleven
Honor

I DON'T WANT TO WEAR the fucking negligée. I want to roll it into a ball and set it on fire.

But I can't do that. My face is still stinging from the slap Don gave me, and I have no doubt he's capable of worse. Much worse. If I don't put it on, he'll probably cart me out there naked.

The outfit cups my breasts perfectly, creating impressive cleavage. It flares out from beneath the bust, but the material is almost transparent. The silky bow between my breasts holds the two sides of the negligée together. I hadn't noticed when Don had first handed it to me, but it also comes with a ridiculously tiny thong, which I've also put on. I figure that some underwear is better than none.

Movement comes at the door again. "You can use the bathroom now."

I grit my teeth. What am I supposed to do? Thank him?

My bladder wants to thank him, however. I'm so desperate now, it hurts, and it's all I can do to stop myself hopping from foot to foot and squeezing my thighs together like a recently potty-trained toddler. I'd threaten to piss in the lingerie, but for all I know, Don and his friends might be into kinks like that.

The lock opens, and I burst out of the bedroom door and head straight to the bathroom without even giving Don a glance. It's partly out of necessity, but also because I don't want him ogling me in the outfit. I don't want to see the hunger in his eyes or find out anything more about what waits for me. For the moment, at least, I'll have a little privacy. The time I spend in the bathroom will delay what happens to me next.

As I'd discovered last night, there isn't a lock on the door. I wish I could put something up against it, but there's nothing I can use. Don can burst in here at any moment, and there's nothing I can do to stop him.

My desperation counteracts any self-consciousness I might be experiencing, and I drop down onto the toilet with a groan of relief. I finish up and flush, and then linger at the sink to wash my hands and face and use the toothbrush that's been provided for me. I rake my damp hands through my hair, trying to tame it into submission. There are red marks on my cheeks where he hit me, five stripes in the shapes of fingerprints. I note that no makeup has been provided for me. They want me bare-faced and young looking. Innocent.

But I'm far from innocent. Not anymore.

I can't help my thoughts going back to the guys. They're never far from my heart. I say their names over and over as though in prayer—Rafferty, Asher, Wilder, Brody. Yes, even Brody. Strangely, I find myself thinking of him the most, wondering how he'll be feeling now I'm gone. He got what he wanted, didn't he? I'm not on the island anymore. Maybe it didn't happen quite as he'd planned, but the result is still the same.

Yet, somehow, I can't imagine Brody is happy with what's gone down, and not only because the others will be furious with him when—or if—they find out. Deep down, I'm hoping this will make him see how wrong he was and that he'll now feel differently about my place on the island with them. It may be too late, though. If Don and whoever his friends are get to do whatever they want with me, the guys might not even want me back. I'll be damaged. Defiled. The thought of putting their hands and mouths on me after Don has done God only knows what with me might disgust them.

That's if I even live long enough for that to happen.

A knock comes at the door.

"Time's up, Honor."

He could just barge his way in here, if he wants, so I go to the door and open it. I haven't heard anyone else arrive yet, but that doesn't mean we're still alone. I have the crazy idea that maybe whoever is coming to the house will be willing to help me, but I quickly quash it. First of all, the last time I tried to get someone to help me, it got that person killed. Secondly, the people coming here are like Don. They're the predators, and I'm the prey.

There will be no help.

I draw a breath and open the bathroom door.

Don is standing in the hallway outside and, at the sight of me, the corners of his lips curl into a smile. "Well, well, well. Don't you look absolutely fucking perfect. Good enough to eat."

I don't reply but stare down at the floor.

"Look at me, Honor," he says. "Don't make me slap you again."

I clench my jaw and force myself to look up.

He grins with satisfaction. "Now say, 'I'm going to be a good girl, Daddy.'"

I mutter it with disgust, but it seems to satisfy him.

"And when my guests arrive," he continues, "that's how you're to address me at all times, got it? You're to be sweet and polite and compliant. Act out, and I'll make you pay."

My eyes must have widened at his words because I see him warm to the idea.

"You wouldn't want me to put you over my knee and spank you in front of my guests, now, would you, baby-doll?"

"No," I hiss.

"No, what?" he prompts.

"No, Daddy."

He smiles again, and something about his face rings a memory inside me.

He's looking at me as though he knows he's won.

His expression launches me back in time, and I find the image of the morning my mother died playing through my head like a movie reel...

I'M SUPPOSED TO BE out for the morning, but I only get a couple of blocks away before I realize I've forgotten my phone. Not having my cell on me feels a bit like leaving the house having forgotten to put my top on, and I know I need to go back for it. My heart sinks. Don has the day off, and he's still

BROKEN LIMITS 105

home. It's one of the reasons I decided to head out for a walk, making myself scarce. I don't really want to go back because then he might ask me what I'm doing and find some reason not to let me back out again, but I also need my phone.

I figure I'll slip into the house via the back and hope he doesn't see me.

I head home and let myself in through the back the door. It leads straight into the kitchen.

Don is standing at the kitchen sink, his back to me. For a second, I wonder what he's doing. The end of his golf club is sticking out of the sink, and the water is running. The tang of bleach is sharp in the air, but there's another scent underlying it—something I can't quite pinpoint.

Curious, I take a few steps closer. There are splashes of red on the draining board, and more is diluted and swirling around the sink with the water.

Is it paint? Why would Don have red paint on a golf club?

He still doesn't know I'm there, he's so focused on the job at hand. There's something strange about the intensity of his cleaning, how his shoulders are bunched, his head bent. Even from here I can see the veins protruding in his neck. The way he's scrubbing is strange, his biceps bulging hugely from the effort.

What could possibly be so important that it needed cleaning with such zeal? Apart from anything else, it's not as though Don makes a habit of cleaning anything, other than his car.

The last thing I want to do is catch his attention. It seems I'm living my life trying to do the exact opposite of that. More and more, I'm trying to make myself invisible, to fade into the background, to become so tiny he doesn't see me. I plan to sneak past and slip upstairs to my bedroom and hopefully escape out of the door again without him noticing.

I edge toward the open archway that leads to the front of the house and the stairwell and freeze.

From the bottom of the stairs, my mother's legs are sticking out into the hallway. They're at a strange angle, her knees bent awkwardly, her feet skewed, and then I realize they're surrounded by a pool of something. It's the same color red as I'd seen Don washing down the sink—shiny and wet.

Forgetting all about Don, I gasp. "Mom!"

I run to her, dropping to my hands and knees in the blood. I touch her arm, and her skin is still warm, but she's just lying at the bottom of the stairs, unmoving, her eyes glassy, staring up at the ceiling.

I scream, "Help! Someone help!"

I don't even have my fucking cell phone on me to call nine-one-one, but I can't leave her to get it.

"Don't worry," Don says from somewhere behind me. "I've already called the paramedics."

As though they could possibly help now.

There is blood everywhere—all over her face, matted in her hair, on her hands, in a pool around her body. Streaks of it mar the walls and floor, as though she's pushed her heels through it, while trying to get up. It's on me now, too—on my knees and palms from where I've been on the floor beside her. I've never seen so much blood.

I'm so shocked and grief-stricken that it doesn't even occur to me to check where Don is or what he's doing. I don't know how much time passes while I scream and wail over my mother's body, but at some point, both the paramedics and police arrive. Strong arms lift me from the floor, but I cry out and struggle against them, not wanting to leave her. I know when they take her away it'll make the whole thing real. My mother will be gone, and I'll never get her back again.

But I don't have either the physical or emotional strength to fight them, and they carry me into the kitchen and deposit me on a chair.

"Let the paramedics do their job," one of the police officers tells me. "You're not helping anyone by causing a scene."

I've been so caught up in my grief and horror that I've forgotten about my stepfather.

"Don?" I say the officer. "Where's my stepfather?"

"He's talking to one of my colleagues about what's happened. We're going to need to ask you some questions, too."

The memory of me walking in to find Don washing off his golf club flashes into my head. Now I'm putting together the red I'd seen him washing off the golf club with the red of the blood over my mother's body.

The truth of it hits me.

"She didn't fall down the stairs. I don't care what my stepfather tells you or what it looks like. Ask him about the golf club. Ask him why he was washing blood off it in the sink when I came in, right before I found her."

The young police officer's gaze shifts away from me uneasily. "This is Detective Don Bowen you're talking about."

"I know who I'm fucking talking about!" I scream. "He killed my mother. That fucking bastard murdered my mother."

Don is back in the room with me, flanked by two of his colleagues.

"I apologize for my stepdaughter," Don says. "She's hysterical after finding her mother that way. She doesn't know what she's saying."

"Yes, I do! I know exactly what I'm saying. Ask him. Ask him about the golf club."

The officers turn to him.

He shakes his head, as if in confusion. "My golf clubs are out in the garage, where they always are."

"Check his hands! Why are they so clean? If he tried to help her, why doesn't he have blood on them?"

"I had to wash them. My fingers were covered in blood, and I couldn't get my phone screen to work to call you guys. I didn't have any choice. If you find any traces of blood in the sink, that'll be why."

I stare at him, understand sinking in, dread causing the world to slow around me, my blood pulsing through my veins like thick sludge. He knows this system. He knows how crime scenes work. He'll have covered every single angle to make sure he doesn't go down for this.

His eyes challenge me to dare say another word.

Nausea and dizziness sweep over me, and the strength goes out of my legs. I land heavily back on the chair and put my head in my hands. I'm shaking all over, and I just want to vanish.

Don killed my mother. He knows I know he killed her.

And he'll do whatever it takes to keep me quiet...

I'M BROUGHT BACK TO the current day.

There was a full investigation, of course, but the coroner recorded her murder as death by misadventure—her falling down the stairs. Maybe she did, but then Don finished her off. The police never believed my story about the golf club. Don simply said I was mistaken. Of course they were going to believe him over me. They always protect their own.

The sound of a car engine comes from outside, and Don glances toward it.

"Ah, excellent," he says, clapping his hands together. "The first of our guests has arrived."

Chapter Twelve
Brody

I'M GETTING IMPATIENT.

I pace the bar, fully aware that I'm getting stares from the bartender and the handful of patrons who've filtered in since we've been here.

"Sit down," Asher hisses at me. "You're making people nervous."

Good. I want others to feel my pain. I want the whole world to feel it.

I can't stop playing the 'if only' game in my head. If only I'd embraced Honor instead of fighting her. If only I'd treated her how she deserved to be treated instead of trying to degrade her. If only I'd trusted the bond between my brothers instead of believing anyone could come between us.

I've been a fool, and I swear, if we get her back, I'll spend the rest of my life making it up to her. I'll treat her like a fucking queen.

But I do what Asher says and take my seat opposite him again.

He taps his fingers on the table and then speaks. "You know why we've been bringing women to the island and paying them to be there?"

I frown at him. "So we can act out our kinks in a safe environment?"

"Well, yes, that too. But it's also been because we were always fully in control of the situation. When we were boys, at Wren's mercy, we had no control over our lives. None whatsoever. So we created the island, where we controlled every little part. We chose the women we wanted. We said who did or didn't get to come to the resort."

I nod in understanding.

Asher continues. "But when Honor arrived, we lost some of that control. She took it from us. She made us open our hearts for the first time since we were young."

"That's what scared me," I admit, though I hate to say it out loud. "She made me feel stuff I wasn't ready to feel. It was easier to see her gone than deal with it."

"And now?" he asks.

I clench my fists on the table between us. "Now, I'm ready."

The door of the bar opens, and I suck in a breath and look over. Sure enough, Don's partner has walked back in.

The fucker had better have something for us. If he doesn't, he may find his face being slammed through the table.

He approaches us, and from the inside of his jacket, he pulls out a paper file. "Remember, this never came from me."

"What am I looking at?" Asher asks.

"It's Don's credit card statement. You're right. He's been busy, but it's nothing more than I would expect from someone on vacation, though I admit, it doesn't look as though he's in

Mexico." He opens the file and spreads out a couple of sheets of printed A4 paper, then he taps his finger to a couple of lines on the statement. "Here. And here, too."

I focus on the printed words, reading the names of the businesses Don has paid money to over the past couple of weeks. Two particularly large sums stand out—the same two his partner, Detective Murphy, is marking out.

A house lease and a car rental.

Of course, the credit card statement can't tell us the location of the property or the registration number of the vehicle, but it can tell us which company he used, how much he paid, and what dates he made the booking.

"I need you to do one more thing," Asher says.

The detective's eyes narrowed. "I did my side of the deal."

"It's not much, but we won't get the information without the weight of the police on our side. I need you to contact these companies and find out where the property is that he's rented and what kind of car he's driving."

"Why would they tell me that?"

"Make something up. Tell them you're his partner, and that you can't get in touch with him, and you're worried for his safety. Maybe he got on the wrong side of a bad guy."

The partner lifts an eyebrow. "Is that a lie?"

Asher pressed his lips into a line and eyeballs the detective. "Believe me, we're not the bad guys here."

I place my fists on the table. "You gonna do it or not?"

He lets out a sigh. "Fine, I'll do it, but then I never want to see either of you again, got it?"

I give him a tight smile. "Not a problem."

He picks up the statement and slips his cellphone out of the inside pocket of his jacket. "Give me a minute."

He steps outside to make the call.

"You think he's going to get what we need?" I ask Asher.

Asher nods. "Yeah, I think so."

Hope rises inside me, but I force myself to push it back down. Even if we're able to find out where Don's taken Honor, we still might not make it in time. It's approaching twenty-four hours since he first took her, and anything might have happened in that time.

Tension fills the air as we wait, but finally the door swings back open, allowing a shaft of daylight and dust motes to appear, and Detective Murphy comes back in.

"Okay, I got it." He puts the file back on the sticky bar table, only this time there is an address written across it. "I want my money now."

We have to trust that the address he's given us is the right one, and not just one he's made up off the top of his head.

Asher is clearly having the same line of thought. "If we find out you're lying to us, we will come back and destroy you. You understand that, don't you? We will make it our life's work to ruin everything you've worked for in your life—your career, your family—everything. We have the power to really fuck things up for you."

He stoops to pick up the bag. "I'm not lying. The address is real."

"The same goes for if you decide to alert your partner. He'll never know from us you gave us this information. If you alert him, your life as you know it is over. Do the smart thing, take the money, and keep your mouth shut." I stare at him as his jaw works.

"I won't say anything. I'm not down with him taking his stepdaughter. We all have our limits."

I give him a curt nod, and he turns and leaves the bar. He might say he has his limits, but I doubt he'd have helped us without the money as an incentive.

I look to Asher, but he's already on his feet.

"That's only a few hours from the island," he says. "It has to be where Don's taken her."

I agree. "We need to call Rafferty and Wilder. If we get on the road now, we can meet them there."

"We can't let him see us coming."

"You think Wren will be there as well?" I ask.

The mention of his name always creates a weird vibe between us. "I don't know, but Rafferty says he's left Reno, so it's a possibility."

The LA sunlight is bright as we step back outside and head to the car. Asher will be driving, so I take out my phone and place a call to Rafferty. I update him about what we've found and then say, "We'll get straight back on the road."

"No, don't," Rafferty says. "I'm sending a chopper for you both. It'll take too much time for you to drive back here and then us fly out together. We'll meet you at a designated spot not too far from this rental house."

"Okay, sounds like a plan."

"Drive out of the city," Rafferty instructs "I'll send you a message with a pin drop location. Meet the chopper there."

"Rafferty," I say, not giving him the chance to hang up. "Do we think Wren is going to be at this same location?"

"Honestly, I'm not sure yet. I have Carter on it."

I'm taken back to my days in the military. "I don't like us going in blind."

"Me neither, but our priority needs to be Honor."

"Agreed."

We end the call.

It's strange how so much of our lives has been focused around revenge and what happened to us in the past. That has changed now. We aren't lost in the darkness of what we've gone through anymore. Honor has allowed us to see the possibility of a real future. A life.

She's become our light.

Chapter Thirteen
Honor

OVER THE PAST COUPLE of hours, more people have been arriving.

I haven't met any of them yet, and for that, at least, I'm grateful. Don has been busying himself with his guests downstairs, while I've been hiding out up here, waiting for the call that will mean the start of this ugly business.

I place my forehead against the cool, smooth wall tile and force myself to breathe. I count as I do so—one, two, three, four—slowly in and out. These men cannot take anything from me as a person unless I allow them to. They cannot change who I am. They cannot change the person I am destined to become. My body is just a vessel in which I reside. That alone isn't what makes me human; my spirit and my will are.

Despite my internal mental reassurances, I can't stop shaking. I'm nervous and jittery and my stomach won't stop churning. I desperately wish I was somewhere else, but I'm utterly powerless to change my situation. I could scream and kick and bite and claw, but they outnumber me. All that will happen is I end up even more hurt. I might even end up dead.

Don's voice comes from the top of the stairs. "It's time, Honor."

My legs feel weak, and I'm not even sure they'll move. He might have to carry me down there. I don't want to be some feeble girl who needs to be carried, though. I want to be strong. I want these assholes to see me as someone they need to be wary of.

I don't want to be a victim.

Despite their reluctance, my feet finally start to move.

Don puts his hand out to me, but I refuse to take it.

"Remember what I told you," he says. "Any bad behavior will be punished."

"Yes, *Daddy*," I say, a cut to my tone.

He doesn't respond to it.

I follow Don down the stairs and into the living room, where I count at least seven men, not including my stepfather.

"Everyone," Don says, gesturing toward me, "this is my stepdaughter, Honor."

At the sight of the men, bile rushes up the back of my throat, and I freeze, my hands pinned to my sides.

They assess me, their gazes running over every inch of my body—arms, legs, breasts, face. I hate to think of the evil thoughts that run through their heads. What have these people done? Who have they hurt in the past to sate their sick needs? They range in ages from early twenties to one man who I guess to be in his late sixties. He hangs back, sitting with one leg crossed over the other, staring at me from behind a pair of designer glasses. His eyes are a pale blue, and when I accidentally make eye contact with him, my heart jolts. He is cool and calm, almost preternaturally so. I see no emotion behind those eyes—no, it's not just no emotion, it's no humanity.

Who is this man?

"How old did you say she is?" one of the younger men asks.

"Seventeen," Don lies.

"She looks older."

Don shrugs. "That's our society these days, isn't it? Kids growing up before their times."

He snorts. "Shame."

"She's innocent, though," Don says. "Untouched. I should know. She *is* my stepdaughter."

That seems to light a fire in some of their eyes, a spark of new interest straightening spines and lifting chins.

I could tell them the truth. I could say I'm older and that I'm far from untouched, but where will it get me? I'm fully aware that my only value is in them believing I'm something I'm not. Without that, what's to stop them just killing me?

Though, by the time they're done with me, I might wish I was dead.

"Let's see the goods, then," a man in his forties says. "That outfit is cute and all, but I'd rather get a look at those tits."

I shrivel inside and fight the urge to hide my body with my arms.

The older man at the back seems uninterested in me—at least not in the way the others are. Why is he here? Is it for Don? Does he want to make sure he's still got the detective's loyalty, or is it the other way around? I'm unsure of the dynamics, but this man exudes power and confidence. It's as though he takes up more space than everyone else in the room.

I wish I understood what the situation was so I could figure out if there was a way I could use it to my advantage.

Don comes up behind me. I freeze, my breath trapped in my chest. Every muscle in my body is a tightly coiled spring, and I find myself squeezing my eyes shut, as though I can mentally propel myself somewhere else.

Rafferty, Brody, Wilder, Asher.
Rafferty, Brody, Wilder, Asher.

I repeat my prayer over and over, using it to draw myself away from this situation.

Don's hand reaches around my body, and his fingers find the silky bow between my breasts. He tugs on one end, and, as I'd expected, the whole thing unravels, and the two sides of the negligée fall open. Though it didn't provide much cover before, my breasts are now completely exposed. My nipples crinkle at the cool air, and I suck in my stomach. My head is bowed in shame. He pulls the rest of the material off my shoulders, and it drifts to the ground and creates a soft puddle around my bare feet. I'm grateful I still have the thong on, but how long that will last, I don't know.

"Come and inspect her," Don offers the men. "Decide how much she's worth."

My head snaps back up. How much I'm worth? What does that mean? Does he intend to sell me?

I'd imagined this situation being that he'd bring his friends over and allow them to have a little fun with me, and then they'd leave. I'd never thought he'd sell me on. What am I looking at? A life of servitude? As a sex slave to one of these men? Somehow, that feels even worse than being in Don's possession. At least I know Don. I can try to predict how he'll react to things. But these other men are complete strangers. I have no way of knowing what they'll do to me, or where they'll take me. What if they try to smuggle me abroad?

The impact of this realization sends the room spinning. If that happens, the guys will never find me.

Chapter Fourteen
Wilder

MY LEG IS BOUNCING as the blades begin to whir. Rafferty is completing the pre-flight checks, and although I'm impatient as fuck to get moving, I let him do his thing. It's not going to help Honor if we crash and burn into the ocean.

Waves of adrenaline wash over me, smashing onto the shores of my nervous system, keying me up. We are going to get Honor back, and what's more, we might also find Wren.

I'm not walking out of there with her stepfather still alive. The man is too much of a menace. We won't be able to rest knowing he's out there, threatening her safety. I'm not sure how on-board Rafferty will be with that, though. He's the one who always has his eye on the legalities.

We've always stuck to the right side of a very thin line in all we do, but we always had the mutual, if at times unspoken, understanding that once we found Wren, all bets were off the table. Well, now the same goes for Detective Don.

Asher will agree with me. Brody, I'm not sure. Either way, even if it means Rafferty banishes me from the island, I'm not leaving Don breathing to keep on threatening Honor.

I'd rather her be safe and never see her again, than have her in my arms every night knowing that fucker could take her again.

My hands ball into fists so tight my short, square nails still manage to dig painfully into my skin. I want to smash that bastard's face in.

"Chill out, Wilder. You'll have a stroke before we get airborne." Rafferty speaks to me via the headsets we are wearing.

The man isn't even looking my way. How does he know I'm freaking out?

The other chopper left some time ago to pick up Brody and Asher. We've arranged to meet them twenty minutes out from the location they found for Don. We can't get too close because the sound of the choppers would alert him, and we're all fit enough to cover the terrain at a jog, even carrying weapons. And we have weapons. Lots of them.

Once we're airborne, I'll check them, load them, prepare them, and make sure we have what we need. That will calm me down some.

The blades start to whine at a higher pitch as they pick up speed. The moment of liftoff is always one I find mildly disconcerting. There are a few seconds of almost weightlessness as your body adjusts.

The chopper jerks and then lurches upward in that drunken manner helicopters have. No wonder some people find them terrifying to travel in.

We gain altitude, the ride smoothing out. We hover for a moment, and then bank as Rafferty heads the bird toward the mainland.

Toward Honor.

AN HOUR LATER, AND the four of us are crouched behind a row of bushes, eyes trained on the building in the distance. It's about ten minutes away, at a slow jog.

The birds are two klicks away, awaiting further instructions.

Now the four of us are back together, I'm feeling more optimistic about getting our girl back. When we split up, I find it disorienting. We are so used to being together and working together.

The fact the rental is in the middle of nowhere presents both an opportunity and issues. Logistically, it's made it harder for us to get to, but once we get inside, no one for miles around will hear the carnage I am about to reap.

"Do you have the flash-bangs ready?" I ask Asher.

"Affirmative," he replies.

The flash-bang grenades will create blinding light and a loud noise, intended to stun and disorient whoever is inside. We need them because we have no idea how many people are in that house. Or who they might be.

"Okay, I'm all set."

Brody glances at us. He's wearing camo and smeared in mud, and he's about to get as close as he can to find out what we're up against. Thankfully, the building is surrounded by a lot of greenery—vineyards stretch for miles around—so he can hide out and get close enough to hopefully get us an understanding of what we're facing.

He adjusts his headset, and then he's off. He moves fast and low to the ground, with an agility that comes from training and years of using his body as a weapon. I've got strength and survival skills, but no way could I approach with such stealth and speed.

The wait for him to report back seems to stretch to an eternity. All I can think about is that Honor is in that house, having God knows what done to her.

Brody feels like shit about what happened. It's written all over his face and in every action he carries out. He volunteered immediately to be the one to go in and get eyes on the place, close up. Dangerous or not, he didn't hesitate. When we get her back, and we *will* get her back, I think Brody will be the one out of the four of us who will be the most determined to make her ours.

He just doesn't know that she already *is* ours. I know it, Asher knows it. Rafferty seems to be catching on, and now it is Brody's turn.

The woman isn't going anywhere. Ever.

The static buzz in my ear is the first warning Brody is about to talk to us.

"There are a group of men in the living room." His voice is quiet, but he's panting a little as if out of breath. "Seven in total, including Don. One in the kitchen, and I think there might be one in the bathroom, but I can't see. I can hear water running, though."

"Armed?" Rafferty asks.

How can he be so calm and analytical? Eight men, at least? What the fuck?

"Are they hurting Honor?" I blurt.

"Not at the moment, but she's…erm…she's being paraded around, in nothing but a thong."

Motherfucker. I'm going to cut his balls off and make him eat them. Don is going to rue the fucking day he came to our island and took what is ours.

"Jesus Christ," Asher snarls. "That's it. We're moving in."

"Hold your horses." Brody sighs. "Let me watch. No one is harming her at the moment, but if they are distracted…by her, then we have a chance of taking them down without her being hurt. Right now, she's in the middle of the room. If we go in guns blazing, she might get hit."

"Are you saying we wait until they're inside her? No. No fucking way." I stand and start moving, but Rafferty pulls me back down.

"We'll move closer," Rafferty addresses Brody over the headset, "but stay two minutes away while you observe. As soon as you give us the go, we'll be there."

"Okay." Brody's voice crackles as the connection dips in and out, but then he's back, clear as a bell. "There's a long rows of hedges to the east side of the house. If you approach in that direction, you won't be seen. If we wait until she's moved off to one side, or is taken to another room, we can go in then. I doubt they're going to keep this configuration they are in for too long. It looks like Don is parading her around to be a prize of some sort. The minute one of the men pulls her to one side for a closer look, or she's taken back upstairs, we go. Two through the front, and two via the door into the kitchen. The front door is likely to be heavily fortified, so we're going to have to go in through the window."

"Right. Two of you through the front window, throw the flash bangs and panic them, and two of us in through the back," Rafferty orders. "We'll move in and wait for your signal, Brody. But if they start to...hurt her, in any way, middle of the room or not, we are going in."

"I don't understand why we can't go in now," I argue. "I go through the window and grab her. If she's in the middle of the room, I know exactly where she is. None of us are going to accidentally shoot her."

"We're probably not the only ones with guns, *asshole*," Brody snaps in my earpiece. "I've been in combat situations and hostage rescue. We go in there right now, there's a huge risk to her if she's in the middle of the group of men. Huge. It's not a movie. You aren't Rambo, despite your size. You can't guarantee to get to her before a stray bullet does. The minute that glass breaks, anyone in there with a weapon will have it drawn and firing. I can't see everyone clearly, as some are sitting, and their faces are blocked from my view by the men standing. I can't judge their age or see who is packing. This needs to be done carefully."

I drag my hand through my long hair and pause at my nape to rub the tight muscles there. As much as I hate it, he's right.

"We give it twenty minutes and see if an opportunity presents itself," Rafferty decides. "If not, we go in anyway."

I open my mouth, but he holds his hand up. "It's settled."

"You know, you might be the boss of us when it comes to the monetary side of things, but you aren't the boss of us when it comes to everything," Brody replies. "Let me say when we go in, Rafferty."

"You already let her be put in harm's way once, and she got taken," I say, not caring if I hurt him. "Now you want to delay again."

Brody's voice comes over the wavelengths. "Yes, exactly because I put her in harm's way before. Because I know what I am doing in these situations. Now, shut the fuck up and get your asses close. There's some movement."

His words stop our arguing dead.

Not waiting to see what the others do, my heartrate kicks up a notch, and I move in toward the house.

Chapter Fifteen
Honor

THE MEN ARE WALKING around me, looking at me as if I'm a piece of meat procured for their delight.

All my plans to seduce Don have come to nothing. There's no hope now. I'll be sold off, and *poof*, I will disappear. Taken away by whoever buys me. Not only will I never see my men again, or the beauty of the island, but I'll be held captive. God, you read about this, don't you? Some woman who manages to break free from a cellar she's been held in for years. Sometimes they conceive children, too.

Bile rises in me, and panic threatens to take hold. That can't be my future. It can't.

One of the men, a dark haired, skinny individual who looks like he's in his forties, with halitosis so bad I can smell him before he gets near, steps in close.

He reaches out a hand and weighs my breast, like it's fruit at a market stall. His fingers are cold, his palm clammy. Then he pinches my nipple, hard enough to hurt.

I don't think but react on instinct. My hand is moving before I can stop myself, and I slap him across the face.

The crack rings out in the room, and I freeze.

He puts his hand to his cheek as if he's been punched by Tyson and staggers back.

He scowls at me. "Not the sort of attitude I'll pay good money for."

The older man speaks. "Oh, I don't know. Isn't breaking them in all part of the fun?" He's the one with the pale eyes and the aura of power. He doesn't move. He's still sitting far back, in the corner. "If you can't get a slip of a girl like this to bend to your will, then perhaps you aren't worthy."

Halitosis guy sneers but doesn't argue back.

"You need to know how to treat her," Don says.

He grabs me by my hair, wrapping it around his fist and yanking so my head jerks to the side. Pain spikes through my scalp, and I cry out. Tears prickle my eyes. I'm completely helpless in his grip, and he drags me across the room, toward a chair in the corner. Don sits and pulls me over his knee.

His hand smooths over my ass, making me want to vomit. "God, you're smooth." He chuckles. "All this lovely, perfect skin, and I'm about to turn it red. I might make you come, too. Just for shits and giggles."

I don't say a word. Nothing I can say right now will work. If he touches me there, I swear that's it. I'll lose it and fuck him up. Even if he kills me, it will be worth it. Now I know he's going to sell me, and I will be long gone before the men can find me, I have lost all hope of surviving. I don't care about that anymore. I just know I won't let this bastard do what he wants with me.

A crack rings out in the room, and it takes a moment for my brain to line the sound up with the burning fire of pain in my ass cheek. *Jesus,* Don doesn't mess around.

Another sharp smack to my opposite butt cheek has fresh tears stinging my eyes. A shadow falls over me, and I glance up and wish I hadn't. One of the men is standing two feet away rubbing his crotch through his jeans as he watches.

"Can I come?" he asks.

"Don't give a shit what you do," Don says. "Just keep it in your pants. DNA and all that."

Oh, my God, they are such freaks.

I try to ignore what is happening, but this is the most humiliating moment of my entire life. Don sets up a rhythm. There are now two men watching. Both of them are rubbing themselves through their pants and making grunting sounds, but I suppose the upside is that they are shielding me from the eyes of some of the others in the room.

"Do you want me to make it feel good for you?" Don asks.

His free hand starts to slide up my leg, and I tense in horror.

"She's got the most perfect skin I've ever seen," one of the men observes.

"Wait until you see her pussy," Don replies. "I tell you, she's worth a lot."

How could I not have realized just how depraved this man was? I believed, still naively, that deep down perhaps he had feelings. Sick and twisted feelings, for sure, but feelings, nonetheless. Instead, Don is purely driven by greed, lust, and his insatiable ego.

As his hand trails toward the top of my thigh, I resign myself to what comes next. Don touching me, and me fighting back and getting myself killed.

A blinding flash, followed by a bang, rocks the room, dulling my senses. I can't see a thing, and my ears are ringing. The world tilts alarmingly, and I realize I've hit the floor. The sound of breaking glass reaches me through the screaming of my eardrums. What the hell is happening?

Another flash, and another bang, and my instincts kick in. I crawl away from the direction of the light and sound, desperately searching for shelter. When Don carried me to this corner, I had seen that behind the chair he seated himself on there was a table. It wasn't very high but seemed to be made of sturdy wood. I reach out with my hand, and when I touch wood, inch myself toward it and try to slide as far under the table as I can.

Pop, pop, pop. The sounds ring out in the room, followed by much louder retorts, with the unmistakable boom of gunfire. My heart pounds wildly, and I struggle to get in enough breath to stop me feeling lightheaded.

Then I hear a voice that takes all my fear away.

"I really wouldn't do that if I were you," the deep voice says.

Wilder.

I would recognize his baritone anywhere.

They came.

I always hoped they would but had started to believe it would be too late. I'm so elated that I don't stop to think about the danger I'm putting myself in as I crawl out from under the table, desperate to find my men again.

An arm fastens around my middle and starts to pull me in the opposite direction. I scream, but a hand drags me upright and slams over my mouth. My heels burn on the carpet as I am hauled out of the room and into the hallway. Here, there is no smoke, and I can suddenly see. I blink my eyes to clear them of the residual sparkles from the flash and wrestle free from the man holding me in his grip. I raise my fist, determined this time I will fight.

"I know I deserve that, but don't knock me out just yet. There's still some fighting left to do."

Brody.

Not caring now about what happened on the island, I drink him in, terrified he's an apparition of my tormented mind.

"It's okay, Honor," he says.

He's really here. I sag against him, and his big arms come around me, holding me up.

"You came," I say breathlessly.

"Of course, we did. We will always come for you. I owe you an apology, but that needs to wait for now. Can you stay out here, please, until it's safe?"

I don't want to stand out here while those men fight for their lives in there. I know, however, that I would be a liability. I don't have a weapon, and even if I did, I'm not an expert at using one. They would be worried about me and put themselves at more risk. So, I do the grownup thing, and despite my desire to help, I nod.

"Good girl," he says. Then he kisses my forehead before disappearing back into the chaos of the living room.

I know I should stay far away, but I need to know what's going on, so I inch toward the door and peek through the crack in the doorjamb.

The smoke is slowly clearing, and what I see turns my stomach. Most of the enemy contingent of men in the room are laid on the floor with their hands over their heads, except for three. Don, who has a gun trained on Asher. A stocky man in his thirties, who has a knife between Rafferty's shoulder blades. Finally, the old man, who has a gun trained dead center on Wilder's forehead.

Wilder has his own gun trained on Don, and Rafferty has his weapon aimed squarely at the older man. Except there's something wrong. Rafferty is level-headed and cool at all times, and yet his hands are shaking.

The old man never takes his eyes from Wilder as he laughs sneeringly. "You can't shoot me, Rafferty, boy. You know you can't. Oh, what?" He gives a mock 'oh dear' sound between pouted lips. "Didn't think I would recognize you? Well, I do. You were always a good boy. It would be such a terrible sin to hurt me. Besides, you and I had such a special relationship. You were always such a favorite of mine, Rafferty. I'm dismayed to see you have fallen so low as to be hanging around with trash like this one here." He jerks his chin at Wilder.

If I don't do something, one of the men is going to be hurt badly, or worse. They came here because of me, and now they are in danger.

"It looks like we have ourselves a regular Mexican standoff here. So, how about we discuss a way out of this?" Don says with remarkable calm. The man isn't even sweating. Whereas Rafferty still shakes as he trains the gun on the old man.

I can't see Brody, and that puzzles me. A moment ago, he was out here in the hallway with me, and he definitely entered the living room, so where is he?

Deciding I can't stand here watching any longer and do nothing, I dart into the kitchen. As silently as I can, I tiptoe around, opening drawers. Finally, I see what I'm looking for. A knife block. I take out the largest one. The big knife is long and ends in a terrible, sharp point. I like the weight of it in my hand, but it's too big and heavy to conceal—especially as I'm practically naked.

I slide it back in and try a different one. This one still has a long blade, but it's the type of knife used for filleting fish and is slender and lightweight.

It will do.

Carefully, I tuck the knife into the waistband of the thong at my back. The thong is fitted tightly, with strong elastic snapped close to my skin, and it manages to hold the weapon in place. I take a few tentative steps, and the knife doesn't fall.

Not sure what my plan is, I nevertheless exit the kitchen and, head high, walk into the living room, creating the distraction I had hoped for.

Brody will kill me if Don doesn't.

"Here she is. The lady of the hour." Don laughs. "I imagine you men are here to save this worthless piece of trash. Well, let me make it worth your while *not* to do so. I'm a very rich man, and I can make it very appealing for you all to walk away right now."

"We don't want or need your money, you filthy pig," Asher spits in disgust.

"It's not only money that I could offer. I have connections, power, and the ability to make your lives golden."

I'm shaking almost as badly as Rafferty is, but with absolute, unbridled rage.

The fear is suddenly gone, like a spell that has been broken. I don't know if it's the presence of the men...*my men*, or the way

Don, even in this situation, manages to be a superior, sneering, overconfident piece of trash. Has the man ever known fear in his life? Possibly not.

After all, if you've gotten away with crime after crime, lie after lie, and harm after harm, you probably think it is going to last forever. I expect even now, Don believes he can talk his way out of this.

None of the men with weapons take their eyes off their targets as I walk into the room. I step forward slowly, my eyes trained on *my* target.

Don flicks his gaze toward me once more, but it's not for long enough. He doesn't look at me for longer than a nanosecond before he's focused back on his target. Wilder, however, swivels to look at me, and his eyes go wide in fear.

The second Wilder is distracted, Don dives to the floor, rolls, and fires a shot at Rafferty.

It misses, but the room once more erupts into chaos. Weapons fire all around me, and people dive for cover. I don't stop. Instead, I speed up and sprint across the room, driven by instinct, not thought. A scream of raw rage tears up my throat, and I'm blinded by my fury. It's as if a primal inner soul is taking control of my actions. I pull the knife out from behind me and launch myself into Don.

I raise my arm holding the knife and plunge it forward as hard as I can. His hands grip my shoulders tight, and Don stares at me, his face turning pale as his eyes bulge. Shocked, I glance down and see blood oozing out all around the blade, which is embedded deep into his stomach.

Oh, my God, what have I done?

He makes a strange, half-strangulated sound, and grips me even tighter. In total shock, I let go of the knife and try to step back.

Something hits my lower leg, and the pain is like a bee sting—searing and sharp Automatically, I lift my leg off the floor, finding it hard to bear weight on it. What the hell? Stupidly, I glance down looking for the bee. I don't see an insect, but I see blood rolling down the outside of my shin.

Next moment, I hit the floor as a heavy weight takes me down to the ground.

"You are so bad at taking instruction." Brody's voice deep in my ear is angry and raw.

"Someone was going to get shot," I say.

He tuts at me. "Yes, you just did."

It dawns on me what the bee sting meant. "Oh."

"Plus, I had my eyes on the situation from outside the room and was about to take Don out."

My answer is drowned out by the retort of gun fire. The air is heavy with a sickly, sweet burning scent.

There is more firing followed by an agonized scream. I try to peer around the immovable force that is Brody, but he holds me down.

"Oh, no, you don't, not again. It's my fault you're here, and I will be damned if you're going to get yourself killed. *Stay low*."

I want to slam my hands over my ears so I can't listen to what's going on in the room around me, but I can't, so instead I lie there as around us a battle rages, and one that I can't be a part of.

Suddenly, as if someone flicked a switch, all goes quiet.

"Fasten their arms and their ankles," Rafferty barks. "Gag them, too."

The weight that was holding me down moves, and I sit. Asher is moving around the room, using zip ties to secure the hands and feet of the men who had been laid on the floor with their arms over their head. He stuffs their mouths with pieces of the men's clothing that he tears from them. Wilder is sitting in a corner, leaning against the wall, holding his side. Sticky red blood oozes between his fingers.

I gasp in horror.

Rafferty has his gun trained on the older man. His hand isn't shaking any longer. Don is on the floor, laid on his side with his legs curled up and his hands grasping his belly. Nausea rises violently within me.

I did that.

I might hate the man, but I've never badly hurt another human being before in my life. His face is a sickly gray, and there is a sheen of perspiration coating his skin.

Brody is standing next to me now, and he leans down and offers me his hand. I take it, and he pulls me gently to my feet. I cry out as the weight goes onto my leg with the wound. I'm still naked, apart from the thong, and I wrap my arms around my torso. There's blood on my skin, and not all of it is mine.

Brody takes off his jacket and slips it over my shoulders. It's huge on me, but that means I can pull it right around myself, hiding my naked form.

He bends down and inspects my leg. "That bullet just grazed you. You'll be fine, but you need this cleaned up and a bandage applied. Thankfully, it didn't penetrate. Unlike Wilder over there. This time, Honor, please stay put. I need to go see to my friend, okay?"

I nod forlornly, guilt eating at me, and shuffle back until I'm leaning against the wall, needing the support.

Asher has finished fastening all the men's ankles and wrists, and gagging them, so now he goes to Don. I expect him to tend to him and perhaps give first aid. I'm shocked when he wraps his fist in Don's hair and yanks his head back with vicious strength.

"Okay, you fucking piece of shit. If you want to live, you start to tell us *now* everything you know about that other piece of shit sitting on the sofa." Asher points at the older man.

I'm confused. Why do they want to know about him?

"As if you're going to stitch me up if I help you." Don gives a raspy laugh.

"Actually," Asher says, "we *will* stitch you back up. I want to see you stand trial for what you've done. You need to pay, and the full weight of the law needs to be applied to you."

Doesn't Asher know anything? I'm horrified by what he's saying. Don will never feel the full weight of the law. He will have a judge in his pocket somewhere. He is corrupt to the core, and clearly has multiple connections that run very deep.

"I think I'd rather die than go to prison, thank you very much. You know what happens to cops in jail." Don coughs.

Asher reaches around with his free hand to the front of Don's body, where he's holding his stomach. With a nasty grin, he presses his hand down hard on top of Don's folded hands. The scream that is wrenched from Don's throat almost sounds supernatural in its intensity.

"Oh, my God, stop it." Don's eyes roll in his head as he drops back down to the floor, except he can't do that as Asher is still holding his head up by the hair.

"I can make it hurt a lot worse than this. I can also leave you to slowly bleed out in agony. Or worse, I can get some dirt and rub it right into that wound, so you die slowly as your flesh decays and infection eats you alive. So, I'm going to ask again, nicely. I want you to tell us everything you know about your friend on the sofa there. Once you finish telling us everything you know, I will clean this up and stitch you back together."

"You breathe a word of this, and you're a dead man anyway," the old man says with satisfaction to Don.

Don's eyes narrow, and even through the pain he must be feeling, I can see him bristling at being told what to do by this man.

"Don't be an idiot and give these fools what they want. They are nobodies. You know the power *I* hold, on the other hand."

"I hold power, too, old man." Don forces the words out as if through a straw.

The man laughs, and that's his mistake. I see the moment Don decides to start speaking. It's not Asher's threats, or even the pain, but it's the old man laughing at him with such a superior tone that pushes my stepfather over the edge. A narcissist to the very end, he can't bear to be made to look or feel small.

"What do you need to know?" he asks Asher.

"Tell me everything you know about our friend Pastor Wren here." Asher jabs his index finger viciously into the older man's forehead. The man stares at him with hate-filled eyes. "I mean, everything."

As Asher turns away from the pastor, the older man lunges forward, but Rafferty raises his gun and pistol whips him around the head. The man staggers back and falls back onto the sofa, cradling his head in his hands.

Rafferty's hands are squeezed in tight fists, and the muscles on his forearms bulge with tension. Wilder, still sitting and leaning in the corner, lets out a weak laugh and shakes his head.

"You're so fucked, old man." Wilder grins, and there's an almost deranged edge to it. "We've waited our whole lives for this moment."

I'm beginning to understand there's something way bigger than these guys just rescuing me going on here.

Just what, exactly, is happening?

I don't get to ask because the door bursts open and two armed men appear, their weapons trained on us.

Or rather, *on me*. What the hell?

"Let me go," the old man mutters weakly, still holding his head. "Or they will kill her."

Wilder lifts his head to the men. "What the fuck?"

"I have a device on me. They are listening in at all times. Good protection knows how to read the lay of the land. I assume they've surmised, as have I, that this pathetic creature means something to you. I suppose now we find out how much. I repeat, let me go, and we disappear. She lives. Or...you can have me, but you don't get her. If you kill my men after, it's too late. She's still dead. You could try to shoot first, but I assure you they are excellent shots. Ex British SAS. The highest trained soldiers in the world, so they say. Dare you risk it? Risk *her*?"

My throat is so constricted with fear it is like breathing through mud. Will they choose me or their revenge?

What if, all along, I've overestimated their feelings for me? What if they are here for him, and I'm merely an added benefit? They get me back for some more fun, and get their revenge?

They look at one another, and Asher nods. Brody dips his head. Wilder hangs his as if he's given up.

Oh, my God. Are they going to let me be killed?

"Get the fuck out of here," Rafferty growls. "We *will* find you again."

"Not in this lifetime." The man stands and wobbles. Neither of the men help him; they don't take their weapons, or their eyes, from me for a second.

When they leave, the pastor shuffling between them, I run to Wilder and take him in my arms. "You need help," I say.

When he looks at me, I'm shocked to see his eyes are glassy.

These men have just given up something at great, almost incalculable, cost to themselves, all to save me.

Chapter Sixteen
Honor

"YOU REALLY ARE GOING to tell us everything now," Asher says to Don. "He's left you here to die, so you owe him nothing. Save yourself. Tell us all you know about Pastor Wren."

Don coughs, and the sound rattles a little, deep in his chest. "Then you'll get me medical help?" he asks.

There's a desperation to his words now. It's as if the closer death gets to stealing him away, the more he fears it. Maybe prison doesn't sound so bad after all if death is the alternative creeping over you?

I don't want him to go to prison, though. He's pure evil, and he'll not stop now until these men are all dead, and I am once more a prisoner, sold off. It will be personal now. I realize with a cold clarity that he didn't come for me because he wanted to sell me, *or* to fuck me. Not truly. He came for me because I got away, and no one does that to Don.

His ego set this whole thing in motion. Selling me wouldn't have netted the man that much money, but it would have been perfect revenge on a girl who outsmarted him and escaped. He's sick and twisted and won't let anyone who makes him look weak or stupid get away with it.

He starts talking, his voice raspy. "I met him a few years ago. He was arrested on some minor charge, but when I started to investigate him, I realized that was the tip of one fucked-up iceberg. I planned on arresting him. For real. The man would have been a prize in my record. My, might I add, flawless record."

"Yeah, we get it, you're a real hero." Wilder sneers.

Brody comes into the room, carrying a first aid kit, and kneels beside Wilder. "Found it in the kitchen under the sink. It's basic but will patch you up for now. Let me take a good look."

He lifts Wilder's t-shirt, and I wince. Brody examines the wound and then moves Wilder forward, who grunts in pain. "Through and through. You'll be fine. Might be tender for a few weeks, as it looks like it's torn through some muscle, but where it is, and the lack of blood loss, tells me it missed anything vital."

"Clean Honor up first," Wilder says.

"Don't you dare," I reply, giving Brody narrowed eyes. "You said yourself, mine is a graze. Treat him, and then me."

"This is so heartwarming," Don says with a sneer. "You found yourself a little family, didn't you, daughter? So, I suppose you weren't lying when you told me what a whore you've become."

Asher digs his fingers right into the wound, and Don screams.

"Say one more word to her, and I'll pull your guts out myself," Asher snarls. "You were telling us about Pastor Wren."

"I've got a file on the man. I can send you it once I'm safely treated and at home." Don is panting heavily, and his eyes roll back in his head.

"Yeah, that's not going to work for us," Rafferty says.

"Send it now. Use your phone." Asher pulls Don's phone from his pocket. "Do it the fuck now, or I swear, I'll pull your guts out so slowly the pain will be beyond anything you can imagine, and I will make it last."

"Just cut his cock off," Wilder grunts.

"Yeah, or I might do that," Asher says with a dangerous grin. "Or your balls. Want to lose your balls, Don? Send us the information, right now. The entire file, and then we call nine-one-one for you and get out of here."

"You'll have to explain this mess and all the dead bodies." Brody grins.

"What dead bodies?" Don glances around him at the men still tied up.

Calmly, as if he's just having a day at the office, Brody goes around to each man and shoots them. One shot, to the head. The men next in line are screaming against their gags, and wriggling to get out of their bonds, but they can't.

I look away, too traumatized to witness it.

"Those dead bodies," Brody says when he's finished.

"Jesus fuck, you're insane!" Don shouts and then gasps in pain. "Do you know who some of these people were?"

"Men who buy and sell women, and that's all I need to know." Brody shrugs.

"You're not going to let me live, are you?" Don's face is a sickly yellow color.

"Send us the file," Asher demands.

Don doesn't move.

Slowly, Asher unzips Don's pants. "I'm really imaginative with a knife, and I can make this slow. One ball at a time. Then your dick."

I swallow. Asher is the one out of all the men I wouldn't want to have against me, not with his sadistic streak.

"Fuck me. Okay, okay." With trembling fingers, Don grabs the phone from Asher and starts to swipe and tap the screen. He's so shaky that he drops it twice, but Asher patiently hands it back to him.

"I don't want to die," Don says. It's almost as if he's talking to himself.

"It hurts, doesn't it?" Asher's voice is suddenly soft, caring. "We have morphine. I can make the pain go away, as soon as you send the file."

Don's eyes flutter closed for a moment.

"Hey," Asher shouts, slapping his cheek. "Don, come on. The file."

His voice is weak now. "I'm trying."

"Try harder."

Asher looks at Rafferty. "Might have to bring the birds in. Got medical supplies. They can land near, lots of open space."

"Adrenaline might wake him up." Rafferty nods.

"Or fucking kill me. Jesus, you incompetents. Hold the phone for me," Don orders Asher.

Asher holds it by Don's face so he can see, and Don manages to swipe and press the screen a few times. "This is the report, in my email inbox. Forward it to yourself."

BROKEN LIMITS

Don hands his phone to Asher. Asher stares at the screen, and then messes about with the phone for a few minutes. "I've sent it. I'll open it and check it's the right file."

Rafferty nods.

"Looks legit." Asher frowns. "Christ, it's a huge file."

"I had everything I needed to take him down."

"Why didn't you?" Asher shakes his head. "I mean, I get you're both pieces of shit, but this could have made you famous. A takedown this big."

"Money and threats, my friend. Oldest trick in the book. The carrot and the stick." Don coughs, and a tiny bit of frothy blood appears at his lips. "He had information on me before I had the chance to come for him. You want him? You better understand that you're dealing with a highly dangerous man. Powerful, too."

"He made you rich and dragged you into his trafficking shit, and look where you are now." Asher laughs.

Don coughs again. "Call for that fucking ambulance."

Wilder's gun is resting loosely in his right hand, which is open on the floor. He's focused on what Brody is doing to his wound.

I glance between Wilder and Don.

Is Asher going to do it? Save Don? He won't go down for this. He will twist his way out of it, and I'll always be at risk. So will these men. They risked everything for me. I can't let them do this.

I grab the gun from Wilder, who shouts as I jerk it from his hands so quickly he doesn't have time to react. Striding across the room, I aim the gun at Don.

"Move out of the way, Ash," I order.

"Hey, Honor. Put the gun down. You don't have to do this," Rafferty says.

"Maybe she does?" Asher surprises me by standing and stepping back. "Perhaps this is exactly what she needs to do. He killed her mother. Kidnapped her. Hurt her. Let her have this." He seems to think of something. "Did he touch you, Honor? Did he hurt you...like that?"

I pinch my lips and heat floods my cheeks. "He didn't fuck me, but he made me touch myself while he watched."

Asher's eyes harden to flint. "Fucking pervert."

"You fucking promised me," Don gasps. "Call an ambulance." His gaze narrows on Asher.

"You know what? I don't think I will. I mean, truthfully, I wasn't going to. I *was* going to let you bleed out, though. It seems your stepdaughter has some mercy in her. This will make it quick."

"Honor, don't," Wilder beseeches me. "He's going to die anyway. You don't have to do this."

I look at Asher, and I can see he gets it.

He shrugs. "It's up to you, babe. In about an hour, he's dead anyway. Painfully, and slowly."

I could leave him to die slowly and in agony. It's what he deserves, but I know something soul deep. I want my face, the face so like my beloved mother's, to be the last thing he sees.

Straddling Don, I aim the gun at his face. A hand gently touches mine, and Asher moves the gun slightly. "Aim for the forehead, baby."

Don's eyes widen. "No, Honor. No. This isn't you. You aren't a murderer."

"Unlike you," I sneer. "Look at my face, Don. Do I remind you of her? Of the woman you brutally bludgeoned? I hope so. I hope so because my face is the last thing you will see."

Before he can beg any more, I close my eyes and squeeze the trigger. The retort isn't loud, but it's powerful, and it knocks me back with force, so I sway and almost lose my footing.

My hands start to shake. Shit, I can't open my eyes.

Someone gently touches my arm, and I flinch. "Baby, it's okay, he's dead. Let go of the gun."

Asher pries the weapon from my fingers and gently leads me away. I'm shivering all over as though I'm freezing. I open my eyes, and I'm not looking at the man I just murdered, but at Asher. The one I thought was the kindest when I first met them is being the man I always thought I saw in him.

His arms come around me, and he holds me close as he strokes my hair. "It's okay. He's gone. He can't ever hurt you again, and you didn't kill him. He was already dead."

"From *my* knife wound," I say.

Asher shakes his head. "Your knife wound, he would have survived. My fingers in there, opening it up, and messing around with his guts, no. I made it a million times worse, and I messed him up inside enough he'd have bled out, or died slowly and horribly of an infection."

I don't know if what Asher is telling me is true, or simply to make me feel better.

"He deserved it, Honor. He was a truly depraved person. Fucked up. Like Pastor Wren." Rafferty is standing by me now, too. "Those kinds of people can't change or reform. They are what they are. You just made the world a better and safer place for many women and girls. Just imagine if he'd found another mother and daughter to terrorize down the line. You'd never have forgiven yourself."

"Who was that man?" I ask.

Asher glances in the direction the older man and his security went. "We all knew him when we were just children. He calls himself a religious man—a pastor—and he took advantage of his position by abusing us all. We've been after him for years."

The news that the four of them were abused as children sends me reeling. As I look around at the four of them, they somehow morph into the boys they were. I picture them young and helpless, abused by some sick pervert, and I want to cry. How could someone have done that to them? I thought I hated Don, but now I discover I have a new person to aim my hatred toward. It also makes me understand why they are the way they are—so desperate for control. They once had theirs stolen from them, and now they live their lives under their own rules.

"I'm so sorry," I whisper.

"What for, Snow?" Wilder asks me from the corner.

"I lost you the chance to get the man you've been after."

"We will get him," Rafferty states firmly. "We have the information we need now, and he won't be able to get away from us again."

"You did that for me." My voice is small.

"Christ, of course we did," Rafferty says gruffly. "You mean everything to us, Honor. To all of us."

Brody ducks his head, but then lifts it again to focus his gaze on me. "Yeah, I fucked up, but when we get you home, I'll make it up to you."

Hope lifts my heart. "Home?"

"Yes," Rafferty says, his voice firm. "Home. Our home, and now your home."

"The island," Asher clarifies.

I blink. "I can stay? Beyond the end of the game?"

"Fuck, yes," Wilder growls. "And we're not playing anymore."

"Do you *want* to stay?" Brody asks, uncertain.

"Fuck, yes," I reply, mimicking Wilder's words.

Asher laughs. "Well, then, yes, you're staying."

Something is still troubling me, and I feel self-conscious and anxious even asking the question. What if I don't like the answer? "What about when the new...you know...new game starts, and the new girl comes?"

"Have you hit your head?" Rafferty asks with seemingly genuine concern.

"I don't think so. Why?"

"Because you're acting stupid. There aren't going to be any other girls. Don't you get it?"

"We let Pastor Wren go," Asher adds. "Our lifetime of work. We let him go...for you. You know what that means? What you mean to us?"

I think so, but I'm too scared to say the words out loud. I'd thought it myself but had been too frightened that I'd never see them again to allow myself to test how it really felt.

Love? Is that what we're talking about here?

"We can talk about this more at home," Rafferty says. "We need to head back and get Wilder properly patched up."

"What happens to all these people?" I point around me at the dead bodies, taking care not to look at any of the faces.

"I have someone who does wet work and cleanup. He'll make this whole scene look like they shot one another. He and his crew will clean it down so your prints and anything linking you to the place are gone." With those words, Rafferty unclips a radio on his belt. "Send in the birds," he says. "Land as near as you can, and let Vadim know, his time has arrived. He and his men need to come in and do their magic now."

A few minutes later, the sound of helicopters approaching has me sagging in relief.

I'm going home.

Chapter Seventeen
Asher

WE'VE BEEN BACK OVER a week, and Wilder is finally looking more like himself. The shot might have gone straight through, but it tore up a lot of flesh and muscle. He still winces when he bends down, but he's been resting, getting some rays, and eating well, and he's a lot more like his usual, sickeningly healthy, robust self. He's even started jogging again. I told him to lay off swimming until the stitches are fully healed due to a slight infection risk.

Honor is fine. Her wound was minor, and Brody cleaned it well, used medical glue and tape, and within a couple of days, she was back to normal.

Well, physically, at least. Emotionally, she seems...mercurial. One moment happy, the next seeming down, the next hyper, and then back to seeming almost depressed. After what she's been through, it's completely understandable, and we're all doing our best to give her what she needs.

"How is it going?" Rafferty walks into the control room and runs a hand through his hair.

"We've had movement," I say.

"What?" He's instantly alert.

"Yeah. A cash withdrawal made from a bank Wren uses, on an island just off Belize."

"Makes sense. When things get too hot, leave the country for a while."

"Yeah, but it could also be designed to throw anyone looking for him off the scent. He could easily have one of his men withdraw that money and leave breadcrumbs for us."

Rafferty frowns. "He can't know we have all his details from Don's file."

I consider what he says. "No, he can't know for sure, but come on. Wren's an evil piece of shit, but he's not stupid. He hasn't evaded the law, or us, all these years by being an idiot. He left while Don was alive, and we were interrogating him. He found out Don had info on him and so paid him off, and he's got to assume we have that info now, too."

Rafferty takes a seat and scrubs his palm over his stubble. He's not as cleanshaven as usual. His eyes are a little bloodshot, too, shadows beneath them. "Do you think he might believe he can buy us, too?"

"What do you mean?"

"Well, here we are trying to track him down, the way we always have. But now, we have email addresses for him, burner phones. Lots of ways of contacting him."

I shake my head. "Why the fuck would we want to contact him? No way. We don't want to give him a heads up. We could lose him forever that way."

"Or...we could reel him in. We email him and tell him we have the file on him. Tell the man we will send it to the FBI unless he agrees to meet with us and compensate us. One of the ways he's avoided scrutiny for all these years is because he has a massive war chest that his faux ministry provides, and he uses that to bribe people."

I scratch my jaw and think about what he's saying.

"All his life," Rafferty continues, "Wren has been able to get away with what he does through a combination of manipulation and money. His experience has taught him that money and power mean you can do as you please. It's also taught him that a lot of people are buyable. Money is the ultimate power because he can use it to get almost anyone to look the other way. Even Don, a man with an ego the size of a small nation, took money instead of fame. He could have been on national television talking about the bust of the century, but instead, he took money. Would it be that much of a longshot for Wren to think the same of us?"

"Except you've already got more money than anyone can spend in three lifetimes," I point out.

"Yeah, you're right."

Then he lifts his gaze to mine. "You don't, though. And you're the hacker." A slow smile spreads across Rafferty's face. "Maybe you're fed up. Sick of the way you're treated as the kid by us. Maybe you're starting to get sick of me making all the decisions just because I control the purse strings. Perhaps, you'd quite like some green of your own."

"Go on," I say.

He's got my full attention now.

"You could contact him, offer him the files, and say you'll wipe everything from our servers if he meets you and pays you. *A lot*. I think he might believe that."

"Then what?" The ways this could go wrong are many. "He's not stupid. He will meet me in a public place, or surrounded by his men, or even send his men instead of himself. He's not going to meet me in the open in the middle of nowhere, leaving himself vulnerable. He's not stupid."

"I bet he'd meet you at his latest church."

I narrow my eyes.

"He's too fucking high on that whole thing. The power of it, the sick thrill. I bet if he thinks he can meet one of his boys in church and corrupt you all over again he'd love it." He makes speech marks with his fingers when he says, *his boys*, and we both shudder. "I think it might be irresistible to him. He's not Don. Yes, he has an ego, but overriding everything, he has a perversion. A desire that he is driven by, despite it being sick and twisted. He risks everything, over and over again, to fuel that desire. He moves and starts out again somewhere new, walking away from money and adulation. Why? So he can start abusing again."

"I'm not a kid, though."

"No, you're not. Out of all of us, though, you look the youngest. And I think if he believes he can take the adult you and do a mindfuck on you again—*win,* as he will see it—I think it will work."

I'm mulling over everything he says. "You know, you might be right. I think, though, we ought to go for the one of us who was his favorite for the longest. The one who he had the biggest fixation on."

"*Wilder.*" Rafferty says the word heavily.

"Yeah, Wilder. Didn't he say it went on for years?"

"Yeah, he did."

I blow out a breath. "And...Wilder is huge now. Massive. He's a million miles from that scrawny boy. Imagine what a kick Wren would get from thinking he's got a man like that to beg him. To go down on his knees for him again, this time for money."

Rafferty twists his lips as he considers this. "I don't know. I still think you might be the better bet."

I shrug. "We can't make a decision about something on this scale without the others, anyway. Why don't we have a meeting tonight?"

"Sounds like a plan. I'm worried about Honor, too," he adds.

"Me too. She's...despondent and then almost high."

"Shock and grief. I expect she's reliving her grief for her mother now that Don is dead. Plus, she's not seen anything like that before—the level of violence."

"Oh, I don't know, she saw her own mother with her head bashed in, bleeding out."

He sighs. "Yes, and that is horrific, but we've piled trauma on top of that. And while Don might not have raped her, what she went through was still abuse, and we know how that feels. I know we had to save her, but hell, it got bloody."

"Maybe she just needs a distraction." I grin.

He frowns. "Or that might be the very last thing she needs."

"Well, why don't we ask her?"

He nods and purses his lips. "I suppose we could."

"Lady's choice," I say.

He laughs softly. "Lady's choice."

Chapter Eighteen
Honor

THE MEAL TONIGHT FEELS different somehow. There's an air of expectation among the men. It weighs heavy in the room.

I don't like the way they've been tiptoeing around me as if I am some Victorian heroine in a gothic novel who has to be treated with kid gloves. I'm okay. Physically, at least. I'm lonely, though.

They asked me to come back to the island with them, and I was excited to be coming home with my men, but now it feels remote between us, as if we are strangers once more. It's almost like the first week here. Obviously, not the same, in the sense that there isn't the hostility from some of the men. However, there is that distance between us once more.

I want that distance gone. I've wondered in the last couple of days if I should seduce them. Maybe they think I'm too traumatized for anything to happen between us. If only they knew that I crave their touch to wash away everything that happened with Don in that sordid rental.

There's a nagging fear at the back of my mind that the issue goes deeper than that. What if they don't want me anymore now that Don has touched me?

I reassured them, Brody in particular as he was feeling guilty, that Don did not do much to me. I didn't tell them about what happened in the shower because they don't need to know. I told them the basics, which is he issued a lot of threats and paraded me around naked in the living room, and spanked me, but I was truthful when I said he hadn't touched me...there. What if they don't believe me?

Or maybe they are the ones who are traumatized. Over the past few days, they filled me in about Pastor Wren and what he means to them. They let the man who tortured them as children—and committed the worst crimes against them an adult can do to a child—walk away in order to save me. Maybe doing so has left them feeling too down on themselves to want anything sexual. They do look tired, and worried. I can see that to a degree they are all in their own heads, thinking constantly.

A new thought suddenly grips me. What if they resent me now that we are back here? Perhaps the reality of their target getting away once more has really hit home, and they're blaming me for it?

I hate the idea that they could resent me for something in such a way, and honestly, I would rather leave the island than stay here as a source of pain for them. Where would I go? I don't know. I'm safe now, though, because Don is gone. Even if I had to start all over again and get a job and work my way up in some organization, or perhaps save until I could go to college, it's not outside of the realm of possibility. I would no longer need to keep moving, always on the run.

"Do you want me to leave?" I blurt the question, almost surprising myself as much as it seems to them.

All four of them stop eating to look at me.

"What?" Asher says.

"I would understand if you did. I genuinely would not blame you. I've stopped you getting the man you've been after for a long time and messed all your plans up. Perhaps the sight of me just makes you all angry."

"Do we look angry?" Brody asks.

I wince. "Truthfully? Yeah, you kind of do. You're all walking around here all scowly and up in your own heads."

"It's funny you should say that," Wilder remarks. "We were just discussing the same thing about you earlier."

"I'm not scowly," I argue.

"No, but you're all over the place." Wilder shrugs. "This morning you were bouncing around happy and excited, and then by the afternoon you were depressed and you went for a nap, and now you're all nervous and overthinking things."

I reach for the glass of white wine by my plate and take a fortifying sip before I continue speaking. "I don't think it's overthinking things if I can sense there's something not quite right between us. You haven't touched me since we got back." There, I put it out there finally. I said what's on my mind.

"Earth to Honor," Asher says. "You were traumatized. We were trying to be gentleman."

I blow out a long sigh. "I don't want you to be gentlemen. I want you to be the men I fell for. I want you to be the men who chased me across this island, and terrified me on one level, but on the other exhilarated me more than anything else has in my life. I miss it. I miss us, and the way you all make me feel.

You said you were bringing me home, and I thought that meant bringing me home for things to go back to the way they were. Not bringing me home to look at me all the time like I'm some delicate flower. If you guys don't want me anymore, I totally understand. I'll leave and not make a fuss. If you do want me, though, what are you waiting for?"

Asher laughs softly. "Well, I suppose that answers our question," he says to Rafferty.

"What question?" I demand.

"We've been feeling the same way," Asher says. "We've been wanting you, but we weren't sure if you felt the same. We didn't want to push you until you were ready. In fact, we discussed today having a conversation with you and asking if you were maybe ready for us to, well, we were going to say *make love*. We were going to try to be gentlemen. It seems you'd rather we weren't."

I pop an olive into my mouth and suck the delicious, succulent flesh. Salt and oil burst on my taste buds, and I chew and swallow before taking the stone out between my thumb and forefinger and placing it gently on the small plate by my side. Then I take a sip of wine and relish the sweet taste of the Gewurztraminer as it glides smoothly down my throat. The contrast between the salty tang of the olive and the sweetness of the wine is delicious.

I look at the men across from me and slowly and seductively lick my lips. "There is a time and a place for being gentlemen. And I would like to experience what being made love to by you four beasts entails. However, I need things to be the way they were." I try to put what I'm feeling into words. "Don didn't touch me, but he treated me like a piece of meat.

He made me feel like I was dirty somehow. The way he paraded me in front of those men and talked about me was so degrading. I know some people from the outside might look at what we do and think it's the same, but it's entirely different. At least it feels that way for me. And that's all that matters, right? I want you to take me every way you can and wash every single bit of my time in that fucking rental house away."

I sit back and swallow past the lump in my throat. It took bravery for me to say those words, and I don't know how the men will react.

"If that's truly what you want, then we are definitely onboard." Wilder reaches across the table and takes my hand in his huge one, dwarfing it.

"You ought to go and get yourself a good night's rest, in that case." Rafferty takes a sip of his own drink, which is a glass of red wine. "Perhaps take a nice long soak in the bath, ease those muscles. Rest up, because tomorrow you're going to be running."

I smile at Rafferty and nod. I wonder if he knows that every night so far Asher has sneaked into my bed and cuddled me close. He hasn't touched me in any other way, except to hold me tight. Would the others mind if they knew?

If we are going to make this a proper thing between the four of us, how will it even work? Would I spend each night sleeping with Asher and only have sex with the other three? Would they want to take turns sleeping with me? Or perhaps, we could buy a huge bed and all fit in it. I almost laugh out loud at the idea. Three of the men are huge, and we'd need something custom made for that to work. Then again, with Rafferty's money, that shouldn't be an impossibility.

"Well, then, gentlemen, if you'll excuse me, I think I will have an early night and prepare myself for the morning."

"That means no sneaking into her bed tonight, Asher," Brody says.

Crap, so they *did* know.

"Spoilsport." Asher's expression grows serious behind his glasses. "Nothing happened, you know. It was just for comfort."

"Very gallant of you." Rafferty rolls his eyes. "Perhaps we need to discuss the sleeping arrangements, as we move forward. Not tonight, though. Tonight, I think Honor needs her sleep more than she needs comfort."

"I didn't say it was for *her* comfort, did I?" Asher says.

His cheeks tinge a slight shade of red, and I'm shocked at what he's admitting. This man who always tries in many ways to be the hardest out of all of them has just openly admitted he has been seeking comfort in my bed. It gives me a warm feeling deep in my stomach. I've been struggling with nightmares since getting back to the island, reliving that terrible time with Don, and reliving discovering my mother's body, too. I guess it's only to be expected, considering everything I've gone through, but it's still not been pleasant. It's been a huge comfort to wake, gasping and trembling, to discover I'm not alone

I smile over at him. "He doesn't stop me sleeping. It's better than sleeping alone. I like his arm around me."

"Maybe some of us would like a turn," Wilder grumbles.

"Right," Rafferty says with a snap of impatience to his tone. "We will have a house meeting tomorrow to discuss the sleeping arrangements. Tonight, let Asher do his usual thing. They aren't getting up to stuff behind our back, and he's not disturbing her sleep. Tomorrow night we will talk about it and figure out a way forward. Is that okay with you, Wilder?"

Wilder sighs but nods. Brody's jaw ticks, but he also gives a reluctant nod, and Asher grins like the proverbial cat that got the cream.

That evening, I take a long, luxurious bath and use the scented oil that was given to me when I first arrived here. Although the scent might have held bad memories for me, bearing in mind it was presented to me by the now ex-housekeeper who made my life hell, it doesn't. It gives me a warm, sensual feeling whenever I smell it because it makes me think of the men and the games we play.

After a soak, I slather myself in body lotion and blow dry my hair straight, so I can pull it up in the ponytail tomorrow. I open the drawer where the outfit that I wear for the games is kept and take it out with slightly shaking hands. I'm excited to be laying these clothes out again, and it feels quite a momentous moment for some reason. I get my boots ready, too, and place them by the clothes folded over the back of the sofa in the living room, and I look at my ensemble for a long moment then head into the bedroom. Next to my bed there is a cool, retro styled radio, with access to all the digital channels. I find something playing some country and let my eyes drift shut to the plaintive sounds of Maria McKee.

I'm already drifting in and out of consciousness when the bed dips gently beside me, and the warm arm wraps around me, pulling me into a solid shape. Asher doesn't speak, which is par for the course. He rarely says anything when he does this. I think at first he thought I was sleeping, and just snuggled up close to me and closed his eyes, falling asleep right alongside me. Every time he's gotten into the bed, though, it has woken me. But I do soon drift back off, his warmth and his scent lulling me to sleep.

Tonight is no exception, and my eyes grow heavy.

THE BRIGHT LIGHT HITS me, and I turn my head away from it. The blinds are open, and Asher is gone. The scent of coffee floats into the bedroom from the living space, and the promise of caffeine lures me from bed.

I head out and discover a light breakfast has been prepared for me and is already laid out. Ever since things went down at the rental house, there is only a skeleton staff running this place now. They consist of the pilot, a handful of security guards, and one man who seems to be working as a butler-slash-waiter. I think this breakfast spread is the work of my men. It makes it all the more special.

There are scrambled egg whites, strips of bacon, and a slice of wheat toast with avocado. There's a card leaning against the coffee pot, and I walk over there and pick it up.

Enjoy your breakfast. It's light on carbs because we don't want you to get a stomachache when you are running. Plenty of protein, though, to give you energy, orange juice for your vitamin C, coffee to wake you up, and a bottle of water to take with you. There's also a prepacked rucksack on the floor by your boots. We hope you're ready for some fun!

I grin to myself and pick up a piece of the perfectly crisp bacon and bite into it, enjoying the satisfying crunch. These men know how to cook bacon to my liking. None of that horrible, soggy, lightly grilled stuff with stringy fat. No, this is perfectly cooked so all the fat has turned crisp and delicious.

When my breakfast is finished, I clean my teeth and put on some simple makeup. I apply a spritz of the scent as a finishing touch. Then I brush my hair until it shines and pull it into a high ponytail. I get dressed quickly and take a look at myself in the full-length mirror in the bedroom. This is the girl I've grown to love. This is the girl I recognize as the new me. I've changed so much in the last month it has been seismic. Even if everything ended between me and these men tomorrow, I could never go back to being that innocent girl I was when I first arrived here. I wouldn't want to, either.

I grab the rucksack and head out of the bedroom. When I reach the living room, the men are sitting around, talking and laughing. When I enter the room, a hush falls over the proceedings.

For a moment, I'm scared they are going to be different with me. Are they going to treat me with the politeness I don't want?

"Well, well, well. Look at you," Asher says with a sneer. "You're back to being dressed the way you always should be. Our own precious little toy. Looks like your tits have grown, too," he says and laughs.

I grin at him in relief. Thank God. I love the more affectionate side of him, but I've grown weirdly attached to the dick side, too.

"Here you go," Rafferty says as he hands me a piece of paper. "We want you to run to the beach today. Which beach is up to you. We are only giving you a thirty-minute head start, then we're going to be right on your tail."

A frisson of fear passes through me. It was on the beach where Don took me. Suddenly, I realize that by playing this game, I'm making myself vulnerable to somebody like Pastor Wren coming for me. This is the absolute last thing I want. I discover there's a big difference between playing at being afraid with the four of them and real fear of someone capable of hurting me.

As if he can read my mind, Rafferty stands and walks to me.

"There are cameras on every single beach on this island now. We've had the whole system revamped, so there isn't anywhere without cover. However, we also got you this." He opens a jewelry box and takes out a thick gold bracelet. "This has a tracker in it," he says. "Once it's locked into place around your wrist, it can't be opened. Not unless you have the key. We will keep the key here in the safe. You can have the combination. We're not trying to make it so you can never take this thing off. But what we don't want is someone else able to take you and get it off. We also invested in a drone defense system. If, for any reason, either we or our security couldn't get to you in time, we have that."

He fastens the bracelet around my wrist and closes it with a snap. Then he takes a small key and turns the lock embedded into the gold. "Now, you'll never be lost to us again."

"What if one of the drones accidentally shoots me?" The idea of drones scares the crap out of me. I also feel mortified that their guards will see some rather interesting things occurring. Then again, I expect Rafferty pays them a hell of a lot of money to keep their mouths shut, and has non-disclosure agreements galore. I'd rather a guard get an eyeful, than someone like Don get near me ever again.

Asher laughs. "They are operated by the guards in the security room. They will make sure they're aimed away from the island to watch for incoming threats only. They won't be watching you or us, unless absolutely necessary."

My cheeks warm. I feel stupid for not understanding that.

"We already had a couple of drones, but now we've got a veritable army of them," Rafferty says. "We're spending over one million dollars upgrading the security on this island. No one's getting to you again. We can promise you that much. We don't want you to feel unsafe, or as if you can never leave the perimeter of the house."

"We've also had a talk," Asher says.

They glance at one another, and then back to me.

"We are going to lay a trap for Pastor Wren. We want the threat of him gone, for all our sakes, and we think he might go for this."

They explain the plan, which entails using Wilder as bait to get Wren to agree to a meet in one of his churches.

"Won't it be heavily armed around him?" I ask, afraid the four of them won't be able to take on all his men.

"He tends to have his personal security, sure. But when he's preaching, he can't have an army standing around. It would freak the people out, and he's new to this place, if indeed he is there. It means he'll want to seem respectable at first. His normal security only consists of a couple of armed men."

"Highly trained men," I state.

I recall Wren saying they were SAS.

"Yes, but so are we," Brody answers. "And we have help. Our pilot is an ex-Ranger, and we have our security, too. It won't be an unequal fight on our side of things."

"Anyway, we need to finalize all of that," Wilder says. "For now, I'd much rather enjoy some time chasing you."

"Right, then. So, you want me to head to the beach?" I smile at them to show my fear is allayed. We all need this, and not to have it marred with worry and doubt.

"The beach, Pandora," Brody says.

"Chop-chop." Asher smacks his hands together. "The clock is ticking."

I mock salute him then head out of the door. The bright sunlight greets me, and I prepare myself for what lies ahead.

A day hopefully filled with torturous fun.

Chapter Nineteen
Wilder

THE OTHERS ARE HEADING in the wrong direction. They all followed Brody because he found footprints, but I quickly figured out it was a ruse. She'd doubled back. I don't tell them, and instead state I will check the other way *just in case*.

I want some alone time with our little morsel.

Asher has had her to himself every damn night, and now I want some time. I won't do anything forbidden, but some touching, that's allowed, right?

In fact, we haven't laid out the ground rules since she's been back. She still has her safe word, but we haven't discussed between us what we can and can't do.

When I get to her, I want to lick and suck her pussy until she's delirious. If I don't taste her soon, I'll explode.

Then, when the others reach us, I will claim first go and stretch that tight pussy wide with my fat cock.

The thought has me stopping for a moment as all the blood rushes south. Jesus, I need to get a grip. I could rub one out right now and still be raring to go, but then I might not get to her first.

I fucking deserve some time with her, after all, I took a bullet. Not that I mind sharing Honor. I'm not possessive over her, and I like to see the other guys with her, but I want to taste her all by myself for once.

My jog isn't going to give me enough time, so I up the speed, despite the twinge in my wound, and run in the direction I believe she's taken. Of course, I could be wrong, and they could be right, Brody is pretty damn good at tracking, himself, but I think my instincts are correct, and she's gone this way.

When I near the beach and see clear, fresh prints in the soil, which is slowly becoming sandy, a rush of victory goes through me.

Yes.

Sprinting down onto the beach, I spot her immediately. She's by the end of the beach, and she's poking her head into a cave. Maybe she is going to hide in there. I stick close to the edge of the dunes, so I can see her, but she won't see me, moving ever closer.

Watching her, I smile when she turns her face up to the sun and holds her arms out. That's my girl—my beautiful, wild Snow. My cock throbs in anticipation, and my mouth waters.

"Thought you could get a heads up on us?"

I swear under my breath and turn to see Brody approaching me, stealthy and silent.

"Fuck me," I mutter.

"They didn't trust you, so I said I'd come and follow you, while they checked out that direction."

"I suppose you're going to be a good Boy Scout and call them."

He grins at me. "I could...or we could have a little fun before they get here. After all, that fucker Asher has been creeping into her bed every night."

"He has."

"Yeah, he has. And Rafferty always has to control everything."

"He does." We're justifying what we're about to do, and I don't care.

"How about we make her come so hard she soaks us both, and then we call them?"

"Fucking A."

We smack hands silently and continue our approach. We are within feet of her before she stills, as if sensing our presence. She can't have heard us, as we're both silent when we want to be, but she turns, and the minute she sees us she runs.

Her legs and arms are pumping, but I cover the ground between us in no time and take her down to the sand, making sure I cushion her fall.

"No!" she cries. "Get off me."

She struggles in my grip, but I hold firm. "You're ours now."

Brody acts as if we're one hive mind, and takes a blanket out of his backpack, placing it on the ground. I lift Honor onto it, not wanting sand getting everywhere, and place her on her back. I straddle her with my big body, pinning her down with my thighs, ensuring she's not going anywhere.

Huge eyes blink at me as she watches me with anticipation. I don't say a word, but rip that damn shirt right off her. I tear the material like paper and pull her bra down, so that her tits are pushed up in it like an offering. Christ, she's got the best pair I've ever seen. And on her tiny frame they are even more luscious.

She gasps at the violence of the action and strikes out at me, her small palms slapping my shoulders.

Good, I like it when she fights. My cock grows even harder, and I growl at her.

Brody grabs her arms and yanks them above her head, pinning her wrists to the ground.

God, she looks like a feast, all for me. I bend my head and suck one plump nipple into my mouth. She moans and half fights to get her arms out of Brody's grasp. In doing so, she pushes her tit farther into my greedy mouth.

I reach down and rub between her legs, finding her clit through her trousers and working her through the material.

It doesn't take long before she's whimpering.

"Suck her tits. I'm going to eat her cunt," I say to Brody.

Moving down her body, I undo her pants and pull them down, revealing the thong she's wearing. I don't bother to pull that down, and instead simply move it to the side, exposing her wet, swollen pussy. She's shaved clean and must have done that last night. She's smooth, and pink, and ripe, and I suck her into my mouth like a fucking peach.

She cries out, and her body thrashes as I suck her entire pussy. I lave my tongue over her outer lips and then push it through them to her clit.

Needing better access, I remove my mouth for a moment and spread her wide with my thumbs, and then I dive back in, flicking her clit hard. I glance up and see Brody pinching her nipples in turn, then flicking them, before going back to pinching them, until they are swollen and red.

Needing to see her come the way I need my next breath, I wrench my mouth from her and spear two fingers inside her. Her channel clenches around me, muscles spasming as she grips my fingers tight. I curl them and hit that spongy spot I know will drive her wild.

Her moans are now cries, and a shadow falls over us. The others are here, but I don't stop. I've not gotten my dick in her, so I am not breaking any rules so far as I am aware, and even if I had, I found her first.

I press repeatedly on her G-spot, and she comes with a scream, soaking me with her juices as she jerks under me.

"Fuck me, that's hot," Asher says.

"I bet you want to fill her with your massive cock and pump her full of your cum, don't you?" Rafferty is breathing hard.

I know all about his kink. He might think we don't, but he hardly hides it. The man gets off on watching almost as much as he does on doing, which is fine by me. I'm not one to judge.

"Want me to stretch her for you with my piercing?" I ask.

"Christ, yes," he says.

Honor herself seems to be floating down on a cloud of bliss so she doesn't add anything to the conversation. Her struggles have stopped...for the moment.

I unzip and pull out my hard dick. I don't want to undress. It feels more raw this way, and raw is what I need.

Honor still seems to be a mindless puddle, so I crawl up her body and position myself at her entrance.

"Wait a minute," Asher says.

Wait? Is he fucking serious. I'm about to turn into the Hulk if I don't get inside her right the fuck now.

"Has she been taking her pill? She couldn't have been while she was...taken."

Well, shit.

"And?" Rafferty shocks me with his words. "She'll look beautiful pregnant."

Oh, no, this is a whole other level. I'm on board for it because I'd love nothing more than to pump her full of my cum and knock her up, but she needs to be too, and at the moment she's blissed out.

"Honor," I say seriously. "Hey, Snow." I tap her cheek gently, and she focuses on me with a dreamy grin.

"That was intense," she says.

"There's more where that came from. I want to do you bare."

"We all do," Rafferty adds.

Shit and double shit, this is getting crazy. I'm turned on, and a bit worried for her, too.

"That's okay, we've done it before. Don didn't touch me. I'm not dirty," she says with a small frown.

My heart breaks right down the middle. "You wouldn't be dirty if he had, but that's not what I'm getting at," I explain. "We want to fuck you. We don't have condoms, but have you been taking your pill?"

She blinks. "Oh. I hadn't even thought about it." Her small teeth dig into her lower lip. "Is it a problem?"

"We're happy with it," Rafferty says, as Brody and Asher both nod enthusiastically. "Question is, are you?"

"A baby?" she says. Then she sighs. "I'd love a baby. I don't have any family."

"Yeah, you do," Asher says. "You have us."

She gives him the softest smile.

"I'm almost due for my period, though. In about a day, so it is unlikely."

"Oh, well, we can keep trying." Asher grins.

I stare at him. Who is this guy, and what has he done with my sullen friend?

"Permission to continue?" I ask sarcastically. Talk about a mood ruiner.

"Take it slow," Honor says. "It's been a while for me, and you're big."

And...just like that, I'm ready to go again.

Slowly and carefully, I push into her, relishing her tightness as my cock forces its way inside.

My breathing is ragged, and keeping this to a tempo that doesn't hurt her is going to be hard.

"God, Honor, you should see your pussy stretching to take him," Rafferty groans.

Jesus. I pause for a moment before I lose it and come.

"Can you take me in your mouth at the same time, Pan?" Brody coaxes.

She nods, and he pulls his t-shirt off, followed by his shoes, which he kicks to one side, and finally he shucks off his pants and straddles her. "Open wide, beautiful."

As she sucks him in and moans around him, I surge inside her, until I'm balls deep and she's gasping around Brody's dick.

Then I really start to fuck her.

Chapter Twenty
Honor

MY MOUTH AND PUSSY are stuffed full, and I don't feel degraded, but I do feel deliciously depraved. This is what I needed, my men, washing away everything Don ever did to me.

Hitching my hips, I pull Wilder deeper into me, seeing stars when his piercing hits my already battered G-spot. Jesus, it is so intense it almost hurts.

He is fucking me like a machine, working his cock in and out, and hitting the right angle to send me over the edge any moment. At the same time, Brody's cock is hitting the back of my throat.

"Fuck, I'm not going to last," Brody grunts.

I'm still momentarily shocked when a flood of cum washes down my throat, thick and salty.

I struggle to swallow it all, and then he's pulling out of me and taking my mouth in a fierce kiss.

"You did perfect," he whispers close to my ear when the kiss ends, words only heard by me, not the others.

I didn't do anything. I'm simply lying here, getting the best fucking of my life. Wilder ought to win an award for it.

He changes his position slightly, and it goes from intense to insane. Holy crap.

"That's it, fill her up with that big cock," Rafferty orders.

I've only just come. Surely I can't again, but it hits me like a tidal wave, washing over me and dragging me under until I can't do anything but surrender. My back bends like a bow, my tits pressing skyward. I squeeze my eyes shut as wave after wave of pleasure rips through me.

"Goddamn, she's coming again." Asher's voice reaches me as if from far away.

Wilder's hips jerk, and he groans as he comes, too. His hot cum floods my channel, and I clench my inner muscles, wanting to hold it inside me.

Wilder sags above me but holds his bodyweight up on his arms so he doesn't crush me. "God, Snow, that was intense." Gently, he pulls out of me, and a heated gush of cum floods from between my thighs. God, I'm wet, so wet, and this is only the start.

Wilder kisses me on the forehead and then climbs off.

It's such a touching gesture, but I don't get time to luxuriate in it as Rafferty pulls me up and turns me over.

"Get on your knees and press your tits to the blanket," he says, his voice harsh with desire.

I do as he says. My knees are on the blanket, and so are my elbows as my shoulders are pushed down, gently but firmly, so I'm in the yoga puppy-dog position.

"Christ, your pussy is so swollen and red, and you're leaking Wilder's cum. Do you need someone to plug you up?"

I whimper when he trails a finger through the mess at my core and swirls it over my clit. "Do you? Honor? Who do you want next?"

"Asher," I say.

I don't really care who comes next, but I know Rafferty will get off on being the last, and Brody has just come.

"Happy to oblige," Asher says. "You want me to do her like this?" he asks Rafferty.

"Yeah, so we can all see her taking you."

"Fucking freak," Asher says, but it's with fondness, not malice.

Rafferty laughs. "That's what makes this so beautiful. We're all freaks one way or another."

He's not wrong. Here I am being taken by four men, one after the other, and I'm loving it.

Asher takes his clothes off the same way Brody did, but he folds his up and places them on the edge of the blanket instead of scattering them all over the sand. I smile at that little detail.

"Do you want me to rub your clit or pull on those amazing nipples while I fuck you?"

"Such a gentleman to ask," I joke.

He smacks my ass hard, and my flesh jiggles. "Enough of that mouth. Which is it?"

"Play with my tits," I say.

"Good choice."

His cock brushes against me, and I welcome the moment he sinks in. Wilder did what he said and got me well and truly ready for them.

"Ah, shit," he groans. "It feels so good to be inside you again."

All I can do is whimper my reply.

He, like Wilder, fucks me hard and brutally, but not so hard it hurts. Instead, it causes a pleasant ache, and a deep sensation of pleasure. His hands reach around underneath me as he plasters his front to my back, and he tugs on my nipples. It's as if there's a direct line between my nipples and my clit, and every time he pulls them, I throb there, too.

I find myself getting lost in a blur of heightened sensation, my body nearly overwrought from the assault on it by these men. I almost zone out completely when Asher's hand moves from my breast and slides across my collarbone to my throat. His fingers tighten around my neck, and he uses his hold on me to pull me up so we're both on our knees. His cock is still deep inside me, and now I'm almost on his lap.

His grip around my throat has startled me back to the present. I'd almost forgotten about this kink with Asher, how he likes to choke while he fucks.

"Careful, Asher," Rafferty warns from above. "She's been through a lot."

Yes, I have, but I also welcome oblivion. "It's okay," I whisper.

His fingers tighten, and my breath shortens. It's like breathing through a straw, and the headiness I'd felt moments before only intensifies. Asher starts to move inside me again, and this time it's with hard, forceful thrusts. My breasts bounce and jiggle, and I can feel the others' eyes on me.

Asher's breath comes harsh against my ear, and he almost growls as his movements become faster. I feel utterly possessed by him, the amount of control he had over me.

My body is his.

It shocks me when another intense orgasm pulses through me, my legs shaking as Asher finds his own release, triggered by mine. He releases his hold on my throat, and I suck in a deep breath, my lungs burning.

Exhausted, I collapse onto the blanket. God, there are two more to go. Suddenly, I don't know if I can do this. I wanted it, but now it feels too much.

"You need a break, sweetheart," Rafferty says. He turns me over and smooths the hair from my face, and then he kisses his way down my body.

When his mouth fastens over my pussy, I whimper. This isn't a break. It's more exquisite torture, and I can't take any more.

"No," I moan. "Too much."

"I'm just cleaning you up, baby," he murmurs against my skin. "You're all messy down here."

The thought is so depraved it has my clit pulsing weakly again. He's cleaning their cum from me. Dear God.

I wonder again if he'd like to do it directly. Would Rafferty like to suck Wilder's cock? I bet he would. Something tells me that Brody and Asher wouldn't be down with playing that way, but Wilder and Rafferty?

Daring to act on my instinct, I moan again and push Rafferty's head away. "It hurts," I lie. "I'm too sore. I need a few minutes."

He nods and wipes his chin.

"If I'm going to take two more of you, I need help getting ready again," I say with a small smile.

"What do you mean?" He frowns. "Do you need a drink? Some food?"

I almost laugh. Bless him, I'm about to ask him for something much more interesting.

"I need to be turned on," I whisper.

He frowns, brows creasing in puzzlement. "I thought I was trying to do that."

"No, not by being touched, I need a break from that. By...watching, maybe?"

"Watching what?"

His face darkens, but I see the way color tints his cheeks. He knows what I am hinting at, and I think he likes the idea some.

"You wanted to clean me, no?"

He nods.

"Why don't you clean me from Wilder?"

"What the fuck?" Brody says. "Honor, we don't play that way."

I sit up and arrange myself with more decorum. "First." I hold one finger up. "I wasn't talking to you." I find myself biting back a smile, enjoying this. If I can face Don, I can face these men and give them—or two of them, at least—what they don't even realize they need. "Second, if I can take all four of you, I think Rafferty and Wilder can have a bit of fun time if it will turn me on."

"Will it turn you on?" Asher asks, with obvious interest.

I'm not lying when I answer. "Yes, it would."

"Why?" he asks.

I shrug. "Maybe I like watching?"

The movie they beamed into my room what seems like years ago now, of the two men, assured me of that.

"If you don't want to...if the idea is abhorrent, you don't have to."

Wilder gives an easy laugh. "It's not abhorrent to me. If I get my dick sucked, it's all good."

Rafferty is glaring at the floor as if the sand has offended him. Shit. I think I've misjudged this.

"Look, forget it. It's cool. Just don't show me gay porn if you don't want to rev my engine that way," I joke, trying to defuse things.

"Would you all think less of me?" Rafferty's voice is quiet but clear as a bell.

"What the hell?" Asher demands. "Why the fuck would we? We're all consenting adults here. I don't want any of yours dicks near my mouth, thank you very much, but let's not pretend we are the most hetero guys in the room. We all like sharing far too much for that."

"No issue from me." Brody shrugs. "If it gets her turned on enough to let me in her pussy, I'm all for it."

Wilder grabs his crotch. "You want to taste Honor on me?" he asks with a cocky grin.

"God, yes." Rafferty sounds almost broken with the desire.

Holy hell, he's been keeping this in all this time? It makes my heart twinge for him. I realize something then. He's always the one who has to be in control. Always. He's the one who the buck stops with, literally and figuratively. He holds us all together, and now we get to hold him.

"Kneel down and clean him up, Rafferty," I say softly. "For me."

Rafferty sinks fluidly to his knees, and with slightly shaking hands, reaches for Wilder, who is already half hard again.

He's so big that even half hard, he's a scarily impressive size. Rafferty leans in close and darts out his tongue, licking the head of Wilder's cock. He flicks his tongue over the piercing and moans when Wilder's slit weeps a flood of pre-cum.

Asher gives a kind of strangled moan and settles back against a tree to watch the show.

Dear God, if I thought I was doing this as a good deed, it has plenty of upside for me because it is the hottest thing I've ever seen. For a man as powerful and in charge as Rafferty to be on his knees for another man makes my pussy clench.

"I can taste you, all over him," Rafferty says as he pauses for a moment, running his fist up and down Wilder's length.

Wilder is totally hard now, and I marvel at his powers of recovery.

"Suck it into your mouth," I say. "The stretch is amazing."

Rafferty does as I say and wraps his lips around Wilder, his cheeks puffing out as he sucks in his massive girth.

"Holy fuck," Wilder hisses. "Jesus. God. Shit. Fuck."

His head drops back, and he closes his eyes as Rafferty sucks him hard and fast, setting up a rhythm, but pausing every now and again to run his tongue all around the thick vein ridging the side of Wilder's cock.

I'm so hot and horny at the sight I reach between my legs and start to stroke my clit.

"Oh, no, you don't. I'll take care of you."

Brody is already naked, and he lies down on the blanket and beckons me. "Straddle me, Pan and use me to get yourself off while you watch the show."

I do. I am dripping wet again, and I climb over him and straddle him. I twist up and down on him, setting up a rhythm and using his cock like my own personal dildo.

"Rub my clit gently," I beg him.

He sucks his fingers into his mouth, wets them, and then does exactly as I ask.

The scene in front of me is so hot, I can't look away. Rafferty moans around Wilder's cock and rubs himself through the front of his pants.

"Take yourself out for me," I say, breathless as I bounce on Brody.

Rafferty doesn't need asking twice. He unzips and pulls himself out, and he's already so hard his crown is purple and shiny with pre-cum.

"Don't come, though," I gasp as my pleasure builds. "Save it for me."

"Christ," Rafferty says, all muffled as Wilder pumps in and out of his mouth.

"I'm going to come," I say with a desperate tone to my words. "Oh, God, I am going to come again." It scares me the way this approaching orgasm feels.

"Come on, Pan. Come all over my cock. Drown me," Brody demands.

I cry out and come so hard I can't hold myself up. I fall over Brody and helplessly grind against him as I come and come. He finds his own release, holding my hips and slamming into me.

God, I'm a wet, stretched, sloppy mess, and I know what I want.

I kiss Brody hard once, and then I get up and walk over to Rafferty and Wilder. "I want you to come in me, as he comes in your mouth," I say to Rafferty.

I marvel at who this bold woman is, and what she's done with the old Honor. I like her, though. We won't always play this way. Most of the time, I imagine Rafferty will direct us like the conductor he likes to be, but today, this is my time to play.

Walking over to Rafferty, I grab the blanket and place it on the ground by where he's kneeling. "Wilder, you need to move to the side, if that's okay?" I ask.

"Yes ma'am." He smirks at me and does as I suggest. He moves to the side and repositions himself, slapping Rafferty's cheek with his cock. Rafferty narrows his eyes at him, and Wilder laughs. "Too far?"

"Yeah, fucker."

I lie on the blanket and say to Rafferty, "Can you hold me up? My legs around your waist while you kneel? You can fuck me while you suck him."

"Yes, I fucking well can. Get closer. I'm about to come all over the place."

"You will be the last one, and then I'll have all of you in me."

He stares at my pussy, a ravenous, pained expression on his face. He hauls me up higher, so my lower half is off the ground, and my legs are held in his arms as he nudges at my entrance with his cock.

When he enters me, he groans and his eyes roll back in his head.

"God, you feel good," I say.

My whole body shivers as he moves in and out of me. It's as if every single millimeter of skin is alive. I'm almost delirious with it.

"Open wide," Wilder says. And Rafferty does.

He opens his mouth and takes Wilder's massive cock in as he fucks me with a speed and harshness that is animalistic. He's rutting me like a fucking dog, and I whimper as he pounds into me.

"Fuck, look at you," Wilder says to me.

I can't speak as I am so lost to this now.

"I'm going to come," Wilder cries, and then he's pumping harder into Rafferty's mouth, who swallows rapidly.

The moment Wilder moves away, his dick sliding out of Rafferty's mouth, Rafferty shouts a strangled *fuck*, and comes in me so hard he pushes me up the blanket with his thrusts.

I'm turned on beyond belief, but my orgasm is weak and mellow, my body too wrung out for anything more.

I collapse onto the blanket the moment Rafferty lets go of me.

He falls onto the blanket beside me and pulls me in close. "You're sleeping with me tonight," he says firmly.

I smile into his shoulder. "Whatever you say. You're the boss."

"Why don't you all get down here and we can have a group cuddle," I say.

"Fuck that," Asher mutters as he starts to get dressed. "That was hot, though. Very fucking hot. Honor, you're going to fit right in. You're as depraved as the rest of us."

"Yeah, it seems we really did open Pandora's box with you," Brody observes. "Just not in the way I had thought."

My eyes drift shut as around me the men get dressed and start packing away, only Rafferty still beside me, holding me.

"Thank you," he whispers in my ear.

I smile and hold him tighter.

Chapter Twenty-One
Rafferty

BY THE TIME WE GET back to the compound, Honor is half asleep. She yawns and excuses herself before shuffling off to her room.

I look to the others. "I'm going to take care of her tonight," I say firmly.

No one argues. I think they all get I need some time to decompress after the somewhat surprising turn of events today, and I don't want to do it alone. I don't want to be around the guys, though, either.

It's not a long-term thing. My masculinity isn't so fragile that I'm going to freak out around them now. I just want a bit of time to get my head around it.

"Okay, boss," Wilder says easily, with no hint of sarcasm.

It seems as soon as that little scene on the beach was over, things went back to how they usually are between us. The dynamic doesn't seem changed.

"I'll go and see if we have any more activity," Asher says.

"Get me if there's any news."

"Of course." He nods once and heads out of the room.

Asher's reaction to today is a bigger worry than my own. I always felt that out of all of us, he's processed the abuse the least well. Will seeing some man-on-man action have freaked him out?

"Will you go and see if he's okay?" I ask Wilder.

He nods and ambles off in the same direction as Asher. Wilder has an easygoing way about him, and maybe Asher will open up to him if he is feeling weirded out more easily than to any of the rest of us.

"At some point, we need to talk about sleeping situations," Brody says. "I don't like us all taking turns with her. I'd prefer we have some sort of situation where we are all together."

"What? Four men in one bed? That will be one snore fest."

He chuckles. "Yeah, but we can work it out somehow. Maybe like, a suite or something, where we have a few beds in one room? Or interlinked? I don't know. Something where she's close to us. I think Asher has been sleeping with her because he's scared that even in this compound, she's vulnerable alone in her room."

I nod in agreement because the thought had hit me, too.

"We can have a talk, include her, see how we want this to work out," I say.

"It's not out of the realm of possibility to find a solution. All it takes is a good architect." Brody grins. Then his face sobers. "Once we find Wren, I'll rest a little easier."

If there's more news on the money situation and Wren's possible whereabouts, it presents a problem. The four of us have always said we'd go after him, but I'm not happy to leave Honor here with all of us gone.

BROKEN LIMITS

Sure, we have good security and can hire more, but I don't trust her with anyone but one of us. We always said we'd do this together, the four of us, but I feel at least one of us needs to stay with Honor. We have new priorities now.

She might even be pregnant with our child soon. One of us. It doesn't matter which, but we can't risk her.

The other option is to take her with us, but again, that puts her in danger, and it means she will see more shit that might traumatize her.

Shit.

I rake my hands through my hair and suck in a long, steadying breath. I love having her here. Hell, I *love her*. It's disconcerting as fuck.

For so long, we've operated in the same way. A band of brothers seeking nothing but revenge, and then a dark-haired slip of a girl came along and changed everything.

The change is good, but it's pulled the ground from under my feet all the same.

Then there was today's little scene. Jesus. It was hot. The hottest thing I've ever done, fucking her while tasting her directly on Wilder.

It fills me with excitement to think about it, but there's also a frisson of apprehension. Where might this lead. I don't mean between any of us outside of play time, but during it, just how wild might we get? It's as if in Honor we've found an accelerant to fuel the fire of our depravity. She's wild, and I have a feeling we're only just scratching the surface.

I reach her room and knock lightly on the door before stepping inside. She's just gotten out of the shower and has a towel wrapped around her body, her hair piled on top of her head so it didn't get wet. Her face is pink and free from makeup, her lashes still damp and clumped together.

I don't think she's ever looked so beautiful.

She sees me there and covers her mouth with the back of her hand as she lets out a yawn.

"Tired?" I enquire.

"Exhausted."

"Let's go to bed, then."

She drops the towel, and I strip of my clothes, though there will be no more sex tonight. We're naked for the intimacy that comes with sleeping with your skin pressed against another person's. Honor is already curled into a C-shape, her back to me, and I wrap myself around her, my body like a human shell.

I gather her in my arms and press my nose to her nape. "You understand that we're going to have to leave soon."

She stiffens slightly against me. "To catch Pastor Wren?"

"Yes. We can't let him get away with what he's been doing—what he still might be doing."

"Hurting children," she says, her voice small.

"That's right." I press my lips to her skin and steel myself for what I'm about to say. "You know I've been doing everything I can to upgrade the security here. You'll be safe while we're gone."

She springs to life, sitting up and twisting to face me. "What? No way. I'm not staying here while you all leave without me."

Tears shine in her eyes.

"It's dangerous, Honor, and if you come, it'll only be a distraction for us. You didn't listen to Brody back at Don's rental, and both you and Wilder got hurt."

"I'll listen this time," she pleads. "I promise. I'll do whatever you tell me to."

"Honor, this isn't about you. This fight between us four men and Wren is between us. Only us." I reach out to place my hand to her belly. "What if you end up pregnant? How do you think we'll be able to function knowing we brought you along?"

She softens slightly and slides down in the bed to face me and tucks her hands under her cheek. She looks impossibly cute, and it makes me smile to think this sweet little thing was commanding me to suck another man's cock today.

"I'm frightened," she admits. "I'm frightened that if you leave without me, you might not come back. What if I never see you again? Any of you. My heart would break."

I stroke a hair away from her face. "We will come back. I promise."

"You can't promise that. I was there at the house with Don. I saw how that went down. What if next time those bodies that are left behind to be disposed of are yours?"

"They won't be," I insist.

She gives a small half laugh. "Stop saying that. You can't predict the future. Stop acting like you can."

"Maybe not, but I trust myself, and I trust the others, too. We've been waiting too long for this to let anything happen."

She thinks for a moment and then asks, "How long will you be gone?"

"I'm not sure yet. Maybe a couple of days?"

Her eyes widen again. "A couple of days? I can't be without you all for that long. It will kill me."

"We'll still have phones. We can FaceTime."

She shakes her head. "It won't be the same, and you know it. If you're going to be gone that long, surely you will be staying in a hotel or something. Can't I come along with you and stay there, instead?"

I blow out a steady breath. "You'll be safer on the island."

"I'll be lonely on the island," she says.

"Better lonely than dead."

I close my eyes and press my nose and lips to the top of her head. I can't stand to see the pain in her eyes and know that I'm the cause of it. What more can I do, though? We can't take her with us, not when there's the possibility of her getting hurt. We've already come too close to losing her, and none of us can go through that again.

She's not going to let me get away with it that easily, though, and she shifts away from me, putting unwanted space between our bodies. She reaches out and runs her fingers through my hair, the feel of her fingers on my scalp sending pleasurable goosebumps across my skin. God, I love this girl.

The knowledge solidifies the determination inside me that I'll do anything to keep her safe.

"Rafferty," she says softly. "Look at me."

I obey her command—I'll do anything for her.

"I'm not going to let this go," she continues. "I understand exactly how you're feeling about me not getting hurt because I feel the exact same way about the four of you. Wilder was shot last time. What if we'd lost him? What if next time, it's Asher who's shot, or Brody, and they're not as lucky as Wilder? I won't cope if that happens. I'll break."

"It'll break me, too," I admit.

She places her fingers against my cheek. "I can't stand the thought of more violence. I know you think it'll make you all feel better, but will it? Killing Don didn't feel good. It still makes me sick every time I think of it. Do you really want more blood on your hands? I can't help but feel there's a better way."

My body tenses at the thought of Wren. "I want him to know who has taken him down. I want to look into his eyes when he realizes this is all over for him and witness his downfall."

"I agree," she says. "You deserve that much."

I relax a fraction.

"But I don't want a repeat of what happened with Don. All those people dead. No matter what they'd done or who they were, that kind of bloodshed isn't good for anyone involved. That kind of ugliness affects the soul. It can penetrate you like something rotten and turn your insides black."

She stares into my eyes.

"So why not do something different? You have all that information from Don, so use it, and not just to find Wren. You have enough to bring him down for real."

I stare back at her, understanding what she's suggesting. Then I touch her chin and kiss her mouth, hard.

"Clever girl. Let's talk to the others in the morning."

Chapter Twenty-Two
Wilder

THE CHURCH IS ONE OF these monstrous modern buildings that's more like a cinema than it is a place of quiet reflection.

We've tracked Wren down to this small town in Georgia. It took us a couple of weeks, but it turns out he owns numerous churches just like this one—including the one in Reno—and likes to move between them. He shows up to conduct a sermon at them like he's a rockstar on tour, drawing huge crowds from his adoring worshippers.

The poverty that surrounds it is sickening. While this huge megachurch reaches high into the perfect blue sky, the homes in the streets aligning it are one story with peeling paintwork and broken fences. It's clear where all the money has gone.

People have come from far and wide to attend, so we're just five more bodies among hundreds, if not a thousand. We might draw the occasional glance, but not for anything suspicious. Wren has his security, but they're with him inside now.

Music and voices filter out through the massive doors.

Rafferty turns to Asher. "Are you ready?"

Asher takes off his glasses, cleans them on his shirt, and then slips them back on again. "Fuck, yeah."

We all clap him on the shoulders, and he gives Honor a brief but fierce hug, and then leaves us to slip around the side of the church. None of us likes splitting up, but in this situation, it's a necessary evil.

Rafferty looks to me. "And you?"

I rub my hands together. "I've been waiting for this moment for almost thirty years."

Our leader focuses his gaze on Brody, but Brody stops him with a lift of his hand. "I'm with Wilder. I've been ready for years."

Rafferty gives a curt nod then slips his arm around Honor's shoulder and pulls her in to kiss her head. "You gonna be okay?"

"Don't worry," she says, "I'll place the call, then I'll be waiting in the car, ready to get you all out of here."

Honor is the one who helped us put this plan in place. It's basically her idea, with a few of our own thrown in for good measure. It's the right thing to do, and it means we've come here unarmed.

We don't need guns. We've got something far more powerful.

I turn to face the church and square my shoulders and straighten my spine. My jaw is clenched, and I can feel the flare of my nostrils. I'm so ready for this.

Without giving the others even a backward glance, I storm toward the building. I use my massive strength to throw open the double doors. They fly apart with force, and the people standing nearby leap out of the way to avoid being hit.

Exclamations of annoyance ring in my ears, but I don't give a fuck. I plan to cause chaos. I want to bring this sermon to an end, and if Wren is forced to do so because of a disruption in his audience rather than it just being me, all the better. Wren has security standing around the edges of the room, and they'll take me down easily enough, but if there's a general disturbance, it'll take them longer to both pinpoint the cause of it and also to reach me.

There's a stage at the front, which Pastor Wren is currently presiding across. It has lights and cameras and a projector that plays silent videos of the pastor preaching his sermons.

The worst—or perhaps best—part of all of this is that the place is packed. It's standing room only at the back. How has he managed to command such an audience?

Desperation. That's what people like Wren feed on. Everyone is lonely and fearful. There's no connection with our community anymore—everyone's too busy online to speak to the person next door. At the same time, the poor are getting poorer while the rich get richer.

We're all just trying to make a connection with someone—with *something*—and in this situation, that connection is with God, or at least the person they view as being closest to Him. They don't know that the truth is this man is the farthest thing you can get from God.

He's the devil.

They're all going to learn the truth very soon.

On stage, Wren has faltered slightly, but he quickly regains his composure and continues his sermon. His voice rings out loud and clear across the crowd, and just the sound of it makes me want to draw blood.

"In today's world," he says, "there are people who will gladly follow a leader until they come face to face with the true cost of their commitment. Our Lord Jesus learned this for Himself, when He came across his would-be disciples—"

I march down the middle of the aisle and shout his name. "Pastor Wren!"

Once more, he hesitates. That isn't the name he goes by now, and to hear it called out throws him. But he quickly finds his place again and continues, ignoring me.

"But when it came down to it, there was a lack of willingness to go through with it. For these people, the price was too great for them!"

"Wren!" I shout again. "Remember me?"

More heads swivel in my direction.

Wren falls silent. His gaze sweeps the crowd, searching for the person causing the disruption. He stops when he sees me, and his eyes widen. He lifts his microphone to his mouth one more. "Security. Remove this man."

I'm putting a lot of faith into the belief that his security won't shoot me in front of all these people. I'm unarmed—deliberately so. My close-fitting gray tee and jeans mean I have nowhere to hide a weapon, and everyone can see that. The security team won't get away with trying to make out like they had to shoot me because I'm armed. A few people in the congregation have taken out their phones and are filming the disturbance. This pleases me, too. I want as many people are possible to see what happens here today, and I hope they're live streaming it to their socials.

I'm nowhere near close to being done. "I look a bit different now than when you used to abuse me as a boy, don't I?"

A gasp erupts from those close enough to hear exactly what I've said. Murmurs of confusion rise from the crowd.

The first flash of panic crosses Wren's face.

I know what he's thinking. First, he'll be considering how many of his security men it's going to take to haul me out of here. His guys are big, but I'm bigger. Second, he'll be trying to figure out how to disparage me. He'll claim I'm a drug addict or a criminal whose word can't be believed.

He doesn't know the show is only just getting started.

Rafferty follows in behind me.

"What about me, Wren? Do I look different than the boy you used to abuse?"

Wren's mouth opens and closes. "Get them out of here," he grits out to his security.

His security team are approaching now, but they're also aware of the hundreds of witnesses. They can't be too rough with us, or it'll get tongues wagging.

Rafferty is different than me. Where Wren might get away with claiming I'm an addict or a criminal, Rafferty is as clean cut as they come. He's in a gray suit and white shirt, and looks every inch the respectable businessman.

Then Brody joins us.

"You abused me, too," he calls out. "It's about time everyone knew the truth about you. I refuse to be ashamed anymore."

Wren pales. "You're all crazy. Get out of here."

"Are we?" says Rafferty.

The giant screen behind Wren changes. It's video footage—terrible, awful, heartbreaking footage. The face of the boy in the video has been blurred out, but the man in it is clearly Wren.

In the audience, someone cries out in dismay. Someone else yells, "What the fuck?"

Wren's face turns puce red. "Turn this off!" he demands. "Turn it off right now."

But his team won't be able to turn it off. Asher has hacked into their video and audio equipment and is controlling what's being shown. The images change, and lists of names and emails start to scroll across the screen.

Others in the audience have aimed their phones away from us now and are pointing them at Wren and the images behind him.

I feel bad for everyone we might be traumatizing, but it's better that than experiencing his abuse for real. Besides, depending on how well they know Wren, I suspect some of them are already more aware of what he's like than they let on. There will already be people in the congregation who are covering for him—or at least they haven't admitted to themselves what he's truly like. But they can't keep their heads in the sand forever, and now they have no choice but to face up to it.

Rafferty raises his voice, ensuring as many of the congregation can hear as possible.

"These are the names and emails of everyone you've been dealing child pornography to. As well as showing them to everyone here, we've also sent this information to the FBI."

This isn't just a handful of people we're talking about—though if it was, it would have still been as important to take them down. No, this is a whole web of child pornography peddlers, the sickest of the sick. There are names people will recognize as well, public figures—politicians and celebrities. It's a worldwide network of these fuckers.

Wren splutters. "I don't know what you're talking about."

"You can't deny it now," Brody says. "We literally have video footage of you abusing boys." He sweeps his arm across the crowd. "All these people have seen it, and I guarantee some of them will have recorded what's happening here on their phones."

Even Wren's security team are looking in Wren's direction. I can tell from their horrified and disgusted expressions that they had no idea Wren was into this kind of thing.

Wren takes a couple of steps back and glances over his shoulder.

"Don't let him leave!" Rafferty shouts.

If Wren runs, we're in trouble, but from the look on his security team's faces, he's not going anywhere. In the car, outside, Honor has already placed a call to the local police to inform them about what's going on inside the megachurch. Wren might have a few local cops in his pocket, but his takedown is so public none of them will get away with trying to help him. If they're seen so much as talking to him privately, questions will be asked.

"You sons of bitches," he spits. "I should never have let any of you live. I should have killed you all when you were boys."

The charismatic, welcoming man of God has vanished. His face is contorted into one of pure rage, and only evil shines out.

A woman in the congregations gets to her feet and points at Wren. "Don't let him leave!"

Someone else joins her. "Don't let him leave."

Then another person and another. Pretty soon, the entire congregation are on their feet, and Wren's own security team surrounds him.

Our job is done.

I glance back at Rafferty, and he gives me a nod. Brody's hand finds my shoulder, and he squeezes. "Let's get out of here."

The feeling is momentous, as if I want to cry and laugh at the same time.

Everyone has forgotten about us now. All their attention is on Wren.

We turn and leave the church, stepping back out into the bright Georgia sunshine. A weight has lifted from me.

There's a chance we'll have been caught on camera and someone might be able to ID us. In which case, we'll have to speak to the police and tell them what we know. I suspect that won't be necessary, however. The proof we've already sent to the FBI and that which will now be shared all over the internet is more than enough to send Wren away for life. Not only that, it will implicate all those he was involved with. Of course, there will be a few of the ring they won't be able to find, but that's only because we've already killed them.

Honor is waiting in the car not far from the entrance. Asher is already with her.

Honor had been right when she's said we could do this without violence, and in doing so we've had far more of an impact. Maybe we'd have taken more personal satisfaction in feeding Wren his balls, but the difference we've made to all

BROKEN LIMITS

the poor abused children—just like we'd been—is far more important.

Besides, we have to take pleasure in how public we made Wren's takedown. Above all else, Wren cared about what people thought of him. Even when he changed names and moved places, he wanted his reputation to be good. He yearned to be worshiped like the God he professed to love so deeply. We destroyed him in front of the people he'd been trying so hard to draw into his spell.

We move at a jog, happy to be away from the place, and jump in the back. It's a squash—especially with me in the middle—but we can deal with that.

"Let's get out of here," Honor says.

Chapter Twenty-Three: Six Months Later

Honor

A GENTLE BREEZE LIFTS my hair, stirring the tiny white baby's breath flowers woven into the dark strands. My feet are bare, and I curl my toes into the warm, white sand. The gentle rush of waves hitting the shore greets my ears, and the scent of saltwater mixes with my now signature perfume.

It's a perfect day, the sun kissing the skin of my bare arms.

A female voice comes from beside me. "I can't believe you live here now."

I turn to smile at Ruth. "I know. Crazy, isn't it?"

"It's like you're one of the super-rich."

I laugh. "Nah, I just live like one."

That isn't strictly true. I have my own money now. Not long after we'd taken down Wren, Rafferty deposited one million dollars into my personal account. I'd told him it wasn't necessary, but he wanted me to have my independence, if I chose it. He didn't want me putting my hand out every time I needed something, or to ever feel like I was bound to them, or the island, purely for financial reasons.

I can hardly believe how lucky I am.

Despite this, a sadness resides inside me that I don't have my mother with me today. She'd have loved to see me like this, though I have to smile at the thought of how she'd react when she realized it was four men I was committing myself to instead of just the one. She'd probably have been a little concerned at first, but would have come around when she saw how completely perfect we all are for each other.

I allowed Ruth to pick out whatever dress she wanted, as she's officially maid of honor for the commitment ceremony. I knew I could trust her taste, and she's dressed perfectly in a blush-mauve A-line gown, with a deep V-neckline. She looks beautiful, but I'm not worried about her turning my men's heads.

I trust them implicitly.

Besides, Ruth hasn't come alone. She's brought the guy from the coffeeshop who she'd been flirting with for ages. Turns out, they're an item now, and I couldn't be happier for my best friend. He seems a little out of his depth, especially when he was met by Rafferty, Asher, Wilder, and Brody coming off the seaplane. I can't say I blame him. They can be intimidating.

It took a little while to explain how our relationship worked to Ruth and her boyfriend, but once I had assured her that I was happier than I'd ever imagined possible, she said she was happy for me, too. I then had to field many, many questions about the...err...logistics of things. I got the impression she was maybe just a little jealous and possibly left wondering how her man might feel about sharing.

"You look beautiful," Ruth tells me with a teary smile. "I can't believe how beautiful. They're going to all be blown away when they see you."

"Thank you."

I feel beautiful, too.

The bodice of my dress is decorated with intricate beading, and the tulle skirt is full length, falling to my feet. The dress is white, though I'm clearly not a virgin. I smile secretly to myself and place my palm against the swell of my bump. It's visible beneath the dress, but it's not like I'm trying to hide it. Everyone knows how pregnant I am, and besides, the guys love it. They can't get enough of me like this and are forever fighting about who gets to feel the baby kick or who gets to lie on the sofa with their cheek pressed to my stomach. We haven't found out if the baby is a boy or a girl yet. I think Asher and Rafferty would both like a little daughter they can protect and cherish, but Wilder and Brody would most likely want a son they can rough and tumble with.

Either way, we'll all be happy to start our not-so-little family. From the way the men have been talking, I highly doubt this will be our only child. If we're lucky enough to be blessed with more pregnancies, I expect we'll fill the island with children.

Needless to say, Rafferty isn't running the resort for kinky businessmen anymore. That won't work when we have children running around. Instead, we're moving the business in a more legitimate direction and running it as a luxury spa option. We still have plans to close it down every so often just for us. None of us wants to give up the thrill of the chase just yet.

"You ready?" Ruth asks, taking my hand.

My stomach flutters with nerves, and the baby gives me a little kick. "I can't wait."

My men are waiting around the corner of the bay. It's been set up with a celebrant to conduct the service—one who was a little surprised at our setup—and I know they're all waiting for me now.

They're all different now. The darkness and intensity that's surrounded them has lifted—though they're all excellent at conjuring it back when the situation desires—and we're all in a much better place.

We learned that Wren died in his jail cell while waiting for his trial. The official story was that he'd hung himself with his bedsheets, but word was that he'd been taken down by others inside. No one likes a kiddie-fiddler, and prisoners aren't an exception.

A floral archway has been set up close to where the ocean meets the sand, so it frames both the sea and the beautiful blue sky. The short but girthy woman in her forties who is our chosen celebrant stands underneath it, and in front of her are my men.

Seeing them standing there sends my stomach fluttering with a combination of nerves and disbelief.

God, they look so handsome. They're all wearing suits, though they've each made their outfits their own. Like me, they're all barefoot—we're grounding ourselves to this earth beneath us, this island that brought us all together. Rafferty has gone for the full three-piece and looks every bit the dashing groom-to-be. Asher has foregone the waistcoat but has his jacket done up, a rose in his lapel. Wilder looks like he's about to burst out of his suit, the pants stretching around his massive thighs. His hair is down, falling around his shoulders in loose waves. Brody is the most casual of them all—with no jacket covering his white shirt, and his dog tags exposed in the open collar—but he's forgone his usual baseball cap. Together, they're breathtaking, and I can hardly believe they're all mine.

Four sets of eyes turn in my direction, and I hope I'm creating as much of an impact as they have on me.

From their expressions, I am.

Rafferty grins. Asher blinks, takes off his glasses to wipe his eyes, puts them back on, and blinks again, as though he can hardly believe what he's seeing. Brody shakes his head, as though in wonder, and Wilder swipes a tear from his eye. A tear? Have I actually managed to bring big, strong Wilder to tears?

I walk slowly across the sand, Ruth at my side. We reach the four men and draw to a halt. I turn to face my best friend, and she gives me the biggest hug, squeezing me close, my baby bump between us. Tears fill my eyes, and I try to blink them away, not wanting to ruin my eye makeup. Not yet, anyway.

"I'm so happy you came," I whisper in her ear.

She hugs me even harder. "I wouldn't have missed it for the world."

She releases me to face my four men, and, despite my best efforts, a tear spills from my eye and runs down my cheek.

Wilder is closest to me, and he reaches out and swipes it away with his thumb. "You'd better stop that," he says, "or you're going to set me going."

I give a laugh. "I saw you a minute ago. You were already going."

He smiles at me as I reach out and grab his hand, gripping his fingers tightly, before letting go.

I move into position, standing so I'm directly in front of the celebrant, my four men around me—Rafferty and Brody to my right, and Asher and Wilder to my left.

"Everyone ready?" the celebrant asks.

We all glance at each other and nod happily.

She begins. "We are gathered here today..."

I miss most of what she says, I'm so caught up in the moment, but then I realize my turn has come, and I need to repeat what she's said.

I draw in a breath and speak, echoing her words. "In the name of love, I, Honor, choose you, Rafferty, Wilder, Brody, and Asher, to be my life-partners, to have and to hold from this day forward, for better or for worse, for richer or poorer, in sickness and in health, to honor and respect, to love and to cherish."

I'm beaming from cheek to cheek, smiling so hard I think my heart might burst. I never even knew it was possible to be so happy, and from the looks on each of the guys' faces, they feel the same way.

"You may now *all* kiss the bride," the celebrant says with a laugh, and then adds, "And what a lucky bride she is."

The men play fight among each other to see who can get to me first and I find myself surrounded, kisses peppering my lips, cheeks, forehead, and neck. I sigh in happiness and almost forget we have an audience until the celebrant clears her throat and we're forced to make some space between us.

"Congratulations," she cries, throwing her arms wide.

Whoops and hollers of happiness fill the air.

Glasses of champagne are brought out by the staff, though I opt for the sparkling apple juice option that's been provided for me. I must admit, I'm looking forward to being able to have the occasional glass of wine with dinner again, though of course my sacrifice will be more than worth it.

Ruth comes up to me and kisses my cheek. "We're going to go back to our room for a bit."

"So soon?" I say, surprised.

She grins. "We want to make the most of that spectacular room, if you know what I mean. And besides, from the way these four men are looking at you, they're hoping for some privacy as well."

My cheeks flush with heat. "Oh, I see."

I've been so caught up in the moment, I hadn't noticed, but now she's pointed it out, I can see they are all staring at me with unbridled hunger. I know a part of it is because my tits are absolutely huge with this pregnancy and my dress shows off the swells of them perfectly. The extra curves I've put on over the past few months have done nothing to dampen their desire for me. They also love that I'm carrying their child. I'm sure they get a kick out of knowing they've got something of theirs growing inside me, even though they don't know who the biological father is. I don't think it matters. We are a team, and they all see me and the baby as theirs.

She hugs me again and then goes to take her boyfriend's hand to head back to the resort. The celebrant is long gone, and Rafferty says something to the remaining members of staff to make them leave as well.

Brody looks at me, and his tongue swipes across his lower lip. "Looks like we're finally alone with our wife."

"So we are," says Wilder. "Though I don't think we're officially married until we've consummated it first."

Rafferty gives a slow nod. "Yes, we definitely have to consummate the marriage."

"All four of us," Asher adds.

A thrill goes through me, and heat gathers between my thighs, my clit pulsing in anticipation. I take a step back and then pause. "There's just one thing."

Wilder cocks his head to one side. "And what's that?"

I toss my bouquet in their direction and throw them a wink and a wicked smile.

"You've got to catch me first."

About the Authors:
Skye Jones

Redeeming dark and dangerous heroes one book at a time.
Skye Jones is an award winning and USA Today Bestselling Author.

She writes dark mafia and contemporary romance as SR Jones, and angsty paranormal romance as Skye.

When not writing Skye can be found reading, dog herding, or watching gritty dramas on Netflix with her husband. She lives in the grey, windswept north of England, which fuels her taste for the dramatic and the gothic.

For a free read sign up for her reader club here: https://dl.bookfunnel.com/ca20ewxx71

About the Authors:
Marissa Farrar

Marissa Farrar has always been in love with being in love. But since she's been married for numerous years and has three young daughters, she's conducted her love affairs with multiple gorgeous men of the fictional persuasion.

The author of more than thirty novels, she has been a full time author for the last six years. She predominantly writes paranormal romance and fantasy, but has branched into contemporary fiction as well.

To stay updated on all her new Reverse Harem books, just sign up to her newsletter and grab a free short story from her Dark Codes series. https://dl.bookfunnel.com/4t79xdwx8m

You can also find her at her facebook page, www.facebook.com/marissa.farrar.author[1]

Or join her facebook group, https://www.facebook.com/groups/13369654796677766

She loves to hear from readers and can be emailed at marissafarrar@hotmail.co.uk.

---

1. http://www.facebook.com/marissa.farrar.author

Printed in Great Britain
by Amazon